The Way Home

A soul-searching journey through chaos

SHALINI MULLICK

Readomania

Readomania
An imprint of Kurious Kind Media Private Limited
readomania.com
email: contact@readomania.com
Facebook: facebook.com/iamreadomania
Twitter: twitter.com/iamreadomania
Instagram: iamreadomania

First Published in 2024 by Readomania

Edited by Indrani Ganguly (Managing Editor, Readomania)

ISBN: 978-93-91800-91-8

Typeset in Palatino Linotype by Shine Graphics
Printed in Delhi

"If light is in your heart, you will find the way home."

—RUMI

Dedicated to my children
May both of you always have light in your heart;
May you always find the way home.

Contents

1

Code Blue

PRESENT DAY

The public announcement system crackled. "Code Blue. Code Blue." There were still 10 minutes before Anya's 8 am shift began but she pushed the croissant back into its wrapper and rushed towards the Emergency Room.

Through the chaos that is usual for an ER, she could see the nurses trying to stabilise the patient who had just been wheeled in—a frail, elderly woman with a loud wheeze. Her lips were discoloured to an ominous blue. The laboured breathing and flared nostrils meant that the patient's airways were already too narrowed for the inhaler that the patient was gripping.

Anya quickly introduced herself and took charge of the situation. It was an acute attack of asthma.

"Dr Anya Chopra. It's my first day today."

"Good morning, doctor. The doctor on this shift was just paged for a procedure."

"Emergency response cart," Anya called.

Anya inserted a nasal canula and reassured the patient.

"We are getting you some oxygen."

The next couple of minutes were critical. If the patient responded to steroids and oxygen, Anya wouldn't need to intubate. She observed closely, not taking her eyes off the patient until the breathing started to settle. In a few moments, the breathing was not as rapid as it had been but the blue tinge on the nail beds was a reminder that the patient had only just made it.

Anya adjusted the oxygen flow and scribbled instructions for steroids to be continued.

Once she was sure that the patient was stable, Anya headed to the nurses' station.

"I am guessing that you are the new doctor from Delhi?" The head nurse, a stout woman, with a long scar running across her left cheek asked. Miriam—her name tag read.

"Yes, Dr Anya Chopra."

"Welcome. I am the head nurse for the ER. Thank you for rushing." Miriam smiled and handed her a set of deep blue scrubs.

"Shall I show you the locker rooms?"

"Yes, please."

Anya followed Miriam into the corridor. Large windows overlooked the symmetrical row of tall coconut palm trees. These trees were a common sight in Goa but getting a view of them from the hospital corridors was refreshing.

At 5 feet 7 inches, Anya didn't need to stretch to reach her locker. She quickly changed into the scrubs. Pushing back her frizzy hair into the plastic cap, she rushed back to the ER to officially begin her new job at Hues of Health (H-of-H).

The patients who trickled in at a steady pace posed familiar challenges. They were a window into a vast variety of ailments—from the life threatening to those that were not critical but still needed immediate attention. Severe stomach-ache, an intense allergy, a broken humerus and a heart attack were the initial culprits. For the last one, she stabilised the patient and called the cardiologist.

"Rodrigues," the genial elderly man introduced himself, before proceeding to prepare his patient for an emergency angiography. She recalled his name from the email exchanges with the hospital. He was one of the hospital directors.

"Good to have you here. I hope you like working here."

"Thank you."

"Please meet Dr Kini and Dr Naik, the other directors, after your shift."

Later, she followed the colour coded signs to the administration block. Compared to the 1,000 bedded hospital she had trained in, H-of-H was smaller, but the sprawling campus was impressive. Cemented paths criss-crossed the lush lawns surrounding the four blocks of the hospital. Teal seashell textured cladding on the main entrance might have seemed frivolous elsewhere, but it was perfect for Goa. It also complemented the neutral beige which exuded warmth instead of the impersonal clinical feel of the white often used in hospitals. Just for a fraction of a second, she was reminded of the similar colour scheme of the brochure of hospital in USA where she had previously applied for a training programme. Then, lest those memories overwhelm her, she forced her thoughts away.

She went to the reception area.

"Hi! I am here for my initiation formalities."

"Dr Anya Chopra?" The young woman in a beige uniform asked.

"Yes."

"Dr Naik is in his room. Second room to your right. And Dr Kini's office is on the 3rd floor. She was paged for a call but should be back shortly."

The sign outside read 'Dr Vijayant Naik. CEO'.

Anya knocked and entered.

The bespectacled middle-aged man poring over sheaves of papers was obviously expecting her. The large work bench on one wall with a huge LED screen gave the room a feel of the control rooms from one of the detective shows on Netflix.

"Welcome to Hues of Health! I see you have noticed my computing stations," Naik said, enthusiastically.

She smiled in response.

"Tech is the future. In medicine too it is a game changer. So is Artificial Intelligence. Hopefully you will get to see how we are applying these at our hospital in due course." He walked over to the armchairs and motioned her to sit.

"Sorry to have allotted you a shift as soon as you arrived. It has been rather busy here."

"No problem. As an emergency physician, the last thing I expect is predictability on the job."

"You have a very impressive bio, especially your publications in international journals."

Anya could only manage a small nod of acknowledgement for this compliment. It had been her sister Zoya's idea that Anya top up her qualifications with the best academic credentials.

"I understand you met Rodrigues already. The third person on our board is Dr Malathi Kini. She would also love to meet you."

Anya took the stairs to the third floor to meet Dr Malathi Kini, the third director of the hospital, who was also the chief of Obstetrics. As Anya walked down the corridor of the Obstetrics and Gynaecology wing, memories of Zoya accosted her senses. Obstetrics had been Zoya's passion. It had been a calling that had manifested early in her medical training. Even the gruelling schedule of the labour room duties had not managed to dim Zoya's energy. Anya had watched how her sister had been touched and transformed by the tender, contended smiles of new mothers and the loud cries with which new-born babies announced their arrival into the world. She wanted to be the doctor who gave the gift of motherhood—an obstetrician. After becoming a doctor, Zoya had taken the licensing exams for USA and moved to Boston to train in Obstetrics. What a lovely life and career her dear sister would have had if fate hadn't intervened.

Anya sighed and tried, once again, to turn her thoughts away from her sister.

Anya crossed the ultrasound scan and procedure rooms and entered Dr Kini's room. There were some magazines and books strewn around on the coffee table in front of her. She glanced through the hospital newsletters, then began leafing through an old issue of an international obstetrics journal. The memories returned, when, unexpectedly, Zoya's name sprang at her from one the pages. It was a research paper Zoya had published a few years ago. Anya could still vividly recall her sister's excitement when it had been accepted, and the celebratory Hot Chocolate Fudge Sundae at Nirula's that had followed.

What a dumb coincidence that she had picked up this very journal to flip through as she waited for Dr Kini, Anya thought as she quickly put away the journal.

"You must be Anya." Dr Kini's soft voice brought her back to the present.

Anya looked up, but her spectacles were fogged up. The familiar wave of tears was building up inside her.

"Thank you for dropping by. I will be with you as soon as I change out of my scrubs."

Grateful for the respite, Anya wiped her eyes and composed herself.

Dr Malathi Kini returned, wearing a long kurta with trousers; her layered hair cut framing her face, and her kohl lined eyes perfectly set in her oval face. The strands of grey seemed to illuminate her clear skin.

"I hope you will like it here. Please sign these joining documents. I will have your hospital email activated shortly."

They chatted briefly about Dr Kini's experience in the Army Medical Corps before joining H-of-H and then Anya politely excused herself.

When Anya stepped out of the building, the moisture laden sea breeze felt like a punch in her stomach. Holding in her emotions had drained her. She couldn't control the torrent of memories, nor her tears. She stood there for what seemed like eternity. The saltiness of the tears that rolled down her cheeks was diluted by the raindrops that had started to fall but nothing could take the sting away.

A FEW MONTHS AGO...

For Anya, random scrolling on her phone was her mind-numbing escape from the real world; an activity that she could do for hours; especially when interacting with people was too tedious and effortful, which, since Zoya's tragic death, it always was. Social media helped to mute the conversations around her. Engaging with virtual accounts was better than being with her family where the stark reality could not be ignored. Posting a status update was so much easier than replying to the innocent "How have you been?" (Was there even a way in which that question could be answered?) Even the trolling and negativity that people complained about were better than the hatred and intolerance in the real world. A world where Zoya had been shot at in a hate crime while vacationing in Florida. A world that didn't make sense to Anya anymore.

Right now, though, quickly changing visuals of the latest reel were not enough to keep her attention away from Subodh's words. Even though her father's voice was almost a whisper, the pain on his face was akin to a shout.

"We lost the appeal."

"What does that mean?" Beeji asked, her gentle voice unusually sharp. But it was a rhetorical question. She already knew what that meant. They all knew. The longstanding dispute between Beeji and her sister for this home had been finally put to rest. More than a decade of visits to courts, numerous sealed letters and notices, and the many hours that Subodh spent huddled with the lawyers—all had come to naught.

Beeji got up from the charpoy with a sudden movement. For her age, Beeji was usually quite agile but right now she grasped Sumita's hand. Sumita quickly steadied her mother-in-law.

"Sumita, please help me to my room." Beeji's quivering voice gave away her anguish.

Subodh, seemingly unaware that his audience had dwindled significantly, continued, "We will need to vacate this house." It had seemed different when the judge had read the judgment. Now, saying it aloud, he felt as he was hearing it for the first time. It also felt heartbreakingly final.

Anya looked up from the phone. She couldn't bear to look at her father; and instead looked around her at her house, as if seeing it for the first time. This small old-fashioned home in Chandni Chowk, where she had lived all her life, was not just her home. It was the abode of so many memories that she had shared with her elder sister Zoya. The news Subodh had brought filled Anya with angst. Was not it bad enough to have had Zoya snatched away from her? Now all those memories that filled every nook and corner of the house were also about to be taken away from her.

Just the thought of having to move out from this house made Anya feel sick. Anya's response to Zoya's death had been to immerse herself in work. But even double duties and extra shifts wouldn't be able to take her thoughts away from this development.

She needed to get away. A colleague had shared a post about a new hospital chain, and she followed the link to the webpage. A 'Join us' window opened and she filled in the fields with her qualifications and experience. It was only when the battery on her phone died out that she realised she didn't know which city the hospital was in. Then she told herself it didn't matter. Nothing mattered anymore.

2

Poached Eggs

Bordello's was Neel's favourite hangout for Sunday breakfast. Neel was one of the few customers who preferred sitting inside over the picturesque patio. Thanks to the glass partition between the cooking and the eating areas, he had the perfect view of the kitchen. Soaking in the buzz and energy of the kitchen was as invigorating as the food which was perfectly punctuated with fresh Goan spices. He often spent his evenings here too, trying out one of the many local delicacies. Recheado, Cafreal, Xacuti and Balchao—he was now familiar with the nuances of Goan cuisine. The buzzing food culture of Goa was the only upside of his having moved here two months ago for his new job. The ledgers and statements that he worked with in the accounts section of H-of-H had already tested his patience. He preferred to think about the balance between chilly and sweet in the Chinese food he loved to cook, rather than the bank balance of his client. So, whenever he wasn't stuck in his tiny cubbyhole office, he checked out the many food joints that Goa offered. The other redeemer, of course, was the beach which was his favourite spot for his cherished pastime—watching clouds. Neel loved to imagine shapes and contours in wispy clouds—from silhouettes of kittens to cotton candy, there was no limit to his imagination. This was a hobby he had picked up as a child. Nina-ma, the elderly caretaker who lived with them, used to run out of stories to tell him while they waited for his parents to come home from work. She would then encourage him to give his creativity a free rein and identify faces or objects in clouds. His interest in those fluffy, freely floating wisps had remained even into adulthood. He always felt better after staring at the clouds that seemed to have a will of their own, and an unhindered freedom that he envied.

"How are the eggs today?"

"Perfect." Neel smiled at Kevin, the chef who had now become a friend.

"I didn't let the water boil over, just as you suggested."

Neel smiled. Poached eggs were something many people could cook, but few could do so perfectly.

The eggs last time had been overcooked just a little. Neel had picked up the subtlety and had wondered how to fix it. An internet search and some experiments in his tiny kitchenette later, Neel had perfected the recipe and shared it with Kevin. Today, with the whites perfectly set and holding the runny yolks firmly but gently, they were elegantly perfect, Neel thought as he devoured them.

His phone rang. A picture of Praveen in his scrubs popped up.

"Dad, how are you?"

"All good, son. Just came back from an emergency call. It was a rather difficult aneurysm, but I could clip it using a new technique."

Typical of his father to always talk about work and his patients. The contrast between how father and son were spending their Sunday morning was also not lost on Neel.

"How is your work, son?"

"It's good, Dad," he replied. He knew that was what Praveen wanted to hear. Besides, Neel really didn't think Praveen would believe it was possible to get bored if you worked in a hospital.

You haven't asked how I was, Neel thought.

But he also knew there was no point in telling his father this. Praveen always used 'you' and 'work' interchangeably. His job was his identity. The brief conversation between them so far was seemingly inconsequential, but it made Neel feel inadequate; as if he would never be able to match up to the stature of his father, who was an acclaimed neurosurgeon.

As usual, conversation between father and son petered down quickly enough.

"Hey, Mom."

"Neel, how have you been?"

"I am fine, Mom. How many more papers have you notched up in those fancy journals?"

Lata laughed. "Just one this month, in *Annals of Cell Biology*."

"Wow. That's fabulous!" Neel knew that the journal was one of the most respected scientific publications in the world.

"How are you, son?" Lata's voice softened to a tenderness that she reserved for Neel. This was a side of her that very few people could access—in her professional life a steely, business-like facade was her best defence. Becoming a pioneer in cell biology in the heavily male dominated world of academia hadn't been an easy journey. But Lata had consistently strived for the best and achieved more than what she had aimed at.

"Doing good, Ma." Neel replied after a very brief pause, which Lata picked up but didn't comment upon. He listened as she shared latest news of his many aunts, uncles and cousins. As a kid, he had spent a lot of time with grandparents and the extended family and had been quite attached to them too. Lately though, he tended to avoid family events. At this stage of their lives, conversations between cousins often veered towards high flying careers, and Neel didn't have much to contribute there. More than a decade had passed since he had finished his schooling, but the aunts and uncles would continue to remark on how surprising it was that he wasn't a doctor. Being the only child of illustrious doctor parents wasn't easy. It was even more difficult when the child grew up to be an adult with an extremely disappointing career.

Neel suggested his parents plan a vacation to Goa before hanging up. Even though Lata assured him they would visit soon, Neel knew it wouldn't be easy to tear his workaholic father away from his patients. He sighed and sipped the fresh orange juice. The pulpiness was perfect, but a dash of black salt would elevate it, he thought.

A FEW MONTHS AGO…

Praveen sliced his boiled egg neatly. Lata passed him the carafe of black decaf.

"Neel is not joining us?"

Lata took a deep breath. Praveen asked the same question every day at breakfast. Instead of replying, she changed the topic.

"Long day ahead?"

"The usual."

Head injuries, complex aneurysms, brain tumours—these were what a routine day meant for Praveen. As one of India's top neurosurgeons, working in Delhi's best corporate hospital, there was absolutely nothing ordinary in the cases that were referred to him from all over the country. But for him, it was all in a day's work.

"How are your cell cultures doing?"

"Hearteningly well."

The satisfaction—and pride—in Lata's voice was akin to that of a mother on her child's accomplishment. And indeed, she was as committed to her laboratory as she was to her son, Neel.

"Great. You carry on to work. I still have my newspapers to read. And hopefully I will get to see that lazy son of mine before I leave."

Lata couldn't fault Praveen for getting irritated with Neel. After all, it was now three months since Neel had resigned from his job, citing boredom as a reason. And he seemed to be making no effort to find another position either. Not that it would be an easy task, given how his resume carried just a BCom degree and had more gap years than actual work experience. If there was one similarity between father and son, it was their stubbornness. Neel had been adamant about dropping out from the master's course that he had managed to be selected for (and which carried a hefty non-refundable fee deposit). His heart wasn't in it, he said. But then, Neel never showed enthusiasm for anything.

"Maybe getting away for a while will help him figure things out?"

"Lata, these are just excuses. You know that there is only one route to success—hard work. Neel is just lazy. And laziness is what makes him the failure that he is," Praveen replied, tersely.

Lata sighed and got up to leave.

Meanwhile, Neel had coaxed himself to wake up early. Praveen was getting testy about Neel's lack of routine, and he really didn't want to aggravate the underlying tension which was now a constant in their home. He walked into the dining area, just as Lata left for work. Praveen couldn't be sure if Neel had heard his comment—but he didn't care. He had meant what he said. Neel was spending all his time loafing around. Looking for a job seemed to be the last thing on his mind. When would this young man develop a sense of responsibility?

Neel had heard Praveen, but he, too, was unperturbed. This was not new. Praveen always told Neel he was lazy and unmotivated.

"Good morning, Dad."

"Seeing you awake early does make for a good morning."

The caustic remark did hurt, but it was still preferable to the usual conversation with his father, which was always about Neel's professional life, or rather the lack of it. Both his parents had scripted stellar careers for themselves; and they couldn't understand how Neel was unable to find stability and direction.

Hoping to dodge 'that' conversation, Neel went to the kitchen to fix himself breakfast. Maybe Praveen would leave for the hospital while he was making his omelette stuffed with spinach and cheese. But luck wasn't in his favour, and he reconciled to getting more of his father's company than he wanted.

"Have you thought about what is next?"

Next—Praveen said it in such a hushed tone, as if there was something to be ashamed of; not worth mentioning in words. Neel's career was always the elephant in the room. After abandoning the MCom course, Neel had struggled both with finding and holding onto jobs.

Not wanting a confrontation, Neel said, "Dad, I have been thinking about it. I want to do something I really enjoy."

"All you enjoy is lazing around. And I don't think that qualifies as a career," Praveen could not keep his tone from being critical.

Neel bit his lip. There was no point trying to speak to the old man.

"Neel, one of my friends is the CEO of a new hospital."

Again, this was familiar turf. His parents, their colleagues and friends were the inner circle, and hot shots of the medical world. But what did all this have to do with him? Except for remind him of that he had failed to live up to the examples his parents had set all their life.

Neel picked at his breakfast.

"They need an accountant. Maybe you should send in your resume."

It wasn't a question. It wasn't a suggestion. It was a statement; one that meant Praveen had already spoken to the CEO, requesting him for a job for Neel. That the decision had been made for him.

Neel's face flushed. It was bad enough not being able to make a career for himself. But getting a job on his father's recommendation was shameful.

"I am forwarding you the website link where you need to send your details. Please don't procrastinate on this." Later that night, Neel had, rather disinterestedly, logged on to the website mentioned in the advertisement to check out the opening. He had uploaded his resume only because he knew that Praveen would keep reminding him about it. Besides, maybe his mother had a point—the hospital was in Goa, and distance from the oppressive ambience of home and his father's presence might help him in figuring things out.

3

Pedro's

After a busy morning shift in the ER, Anya had gone to the wards to check on some patients. By the time she returned to the Residences Block, it was nearing evening. She was heading upstairs to her apartment when she heard the sizzle of frying from the dining hall. The fragrance of spicy hot oil followed, and she peeped through the dining hall window. As she had expected, the cook was deep frying fritters in a large *kadhai*. The dining hall was crowded, but she managed to find herself one of the last few empty seats.

"Pakora, ma'am?" the server asked.

"Yes, and masala chai please."

The crispy fritters arrived almost instantly. She picked up one and blew gently to cool it.

"Can I take this seat?" A tall, lanky youth wearing distressed jeans and a deep blue t-shirt, holding a can of Diet Coke asked.

"Sure."

"Neel Sahay," he introduced himself.

"Anya Chopra."

Neel's platter also arrived. Before picking up one of the tempting pakoras, he carefully arranged the fritters symmetrically around the tiny bowl of bright green chutney. He liked his food to be Instaworthy too.

Anya, on the other hand, handpicked each cauliflower pakora from her plate and pushed them to a side. She picked at a round pakora—potato—with her fingers.

"Don't you like cauliflower?" Neel asked.

Anya nodded without looking up, fighting back tears. How could she tell him that cauliflower was actually her favourite variety? That Zoya always kept her share of cauliflower pakoras for her kid sister? And that in the unpredictable Delhi monsoons, Zoya would pester Beeji to make the girls a batch of cauliflower pakoras which the girls would enjoy as they took in the earthy smell of the rain. The memory was so vivid that she could have sworn that the smell of hot oil had been replaced by petrichor.

Anya shook her head, trying to dismiss the image of Zoya that was building up in her head.

She reminded herself that she was sharing her table with someone, and he was saying something to her. She tried to pay attention.

"I haven't seen you around. Have you joined recently? Or are you a guest, waiting for someone?" Neel had noted Anya's distraction and gently nudged her back into the present.

"I am an emergency physician. I joined recently. I haven't had much time to explore the area."

"It is a lovely campus. You must check it out."

Neel slowly munched through his fritters and called for another Diet Coke.

"You must be a surgeon—neuro or ortho?" It was Anya's turn now.

This was a common guessing game played consciously and subconsciously in hospitals every day. Match the personality-persona of a doctor to the possible area of specialisation. Anya waited for Neel to answer as she took a sip of the tea.

Neel's face darkened a bit. That was the thing with doctors, he thought. They assumed everyone was, wanted to be, or should be a doctor. They simply couldn't see beyond medicine.

"There are other things to life than medicine. More interesting things," Neel said, somewhat rudely, Anya thought. She opened her mouth for a retort, but decided to keep silent. Neel continued crunching on the pakoras. Anya let the warmth of her tea seep through to her fingers through the glass tumbler, waiting for it to cool a little more.

After a while, Neel pushed the plate away. "I am sorry. That was rude of me," he said.

"That's ok," Anya said, avoiding his gaze.

"No really, I apologise. It's just that…" Neel fumbled for words. Anya realised he wasn't being arrogant. On the contrary he looked a little lost, as if beseeching her to understand. She smiled, instantly making him more comfortable.

He continued. "My parents are doctors, pretty renowned ones, in fact. All my life, I have had to deal with the expectations of following in their footsteps."

"And…?"

Anya sensed there was more coming and waited. But Neel surprised her with a counter-question.

"Why would you think I am a surgeon?"

"They have the maximum caffeine requirements in the hospital." Anya looked at the can of soda in front of him.

Neel managed a smile—this was an unexpected explanation. And one that certainly had nothing to do with his parents, or the comparisons that always burdened him.

"I am not a doctor. I work in accounts."

"Oh, okay. Have you been here long?"

"Almost two months."

"Can you help me with something?" Anya asked.

"Sure, as long it's not related to patients." He grinned.

"The AC in my room isn't working. Whom do I call to have it fixed?"

"Download the H-of-H app. It's pretty useful."

The logo of the hospital showed up on Playstore.

Duty schedules, events, help section and contacts—everything was laid out systematically.

"Be warned though. There is still some stuff that the app cannot help you out with."

"Like what?"

"Like it won't tell you about the best seafood joints around, or that Pedro's store just outside the main gate is where everyone stocks up on grocery."

Anya laughed. "I guess I will have to take your help for those."

"Sure. I am heading out to Pedro's right now. You can come with me if you like."

They walked through the lawns which bore a rain-washed freshness. The dense green shrubbery was dotted with the white and purple of the cockscomb. Neel led Anya outside the hospital gates, to a shop with the signboard 'Pedro's'. 'I love Goa' T-shirts and sunhats hung on metal racks outside. The small store front led to well stocked aisles inside.

"Hi Pedro! This is Dr Anya. She has joined the hospital recently. I insisted that she check out your tuck shop."

"Thank you, Neel. Welcome Doctor." Pedro, a broad-shouldered man with a handlebar moustache and large aviator sunglasses, waved genially in the direction of the aisle.

Neel always enjoyed conversations with Pedro, especially his warm, throaty laughter. He hoped that with the hospital expanding its operations, business for the store would improve too. Sightless Pedro and his daughter Grace needed all the support that they could get.

Neel bagged several beer and soda cans and packets of savoury snacks.

Anya returned to the cash counter with her stock of cereal, milk and instant noodles.

"Hello doctor, I am Grace. If you need any items for cooking, we can arrange those too."

"Hmm. Some frozen kebabs would be good."

"Sure. I will send these bags to your rooms."

Anya scribbled her room number.

"Doctor, if you need motorcycle rentals, I will arrange the best discounts for you," Pedro called out.

Neel and Anya began walking back towards the hospital.

"Where is the closest beach?"

"Just a 10-minute walk after the first right down this road."

"Thanks. Maybe I will check it out now."

"Hmm, the high tide during monsoon can be unpredictable, and the beaches close early. But I suppose you could squeeze in a short visit before sunset."

"It might rain though," she said sceptically, looking at the overcast sky above; and for excuses to go back to her room.

Neel frowned.

"That's a stratus; and they don't usually bring rain."

"That's a what?"

"The cloud," Neel replied, impatiently.

"Oh! I don't know much about clouds."

Of course! Doctors hardly have time or interest in anything other than their work, thought Neel to himself.

"So, you like studying clouds?"

"Yeah, I love looking at the clouds—analysing their shapes, and the patterns they make. I guess you think it's weird?" Neel asked cautiously.

My sister loved to study the stars and constellations, Anya bit her lip to stop the words from coming out. Zoya loved stargazing. HAD loved stargazing.

"Not really," she managed to say instead, before taking the small right turn that Neel had directed her towards.

Neel walked back to the hospital. The silence that had ensued after he had mentioned his love for clouds to Anya was not unexpected. Most people didn't understand Neel's unusual hobby, and he preferred keeping silent over explaining his interests. Same with conversations around his career. H-of-H was his fourth job in three years. The work wasn't bad; and the management was great too, but something was missing. This wasn't what he wanted to spend a lifetime doing. What truly excited him, ignited his passion was the culinary arts. Even as a child, he loved to watch their house help cook. He had always found the kitchen to be a wondrous place. But becoming a chef wasn't as awe inspiring a career as medicine.

Anya didn't really want to go to the beach, but it was the thought of Beeji's gentle admonishments that had prompted her to venture outside the hospital campus.

Whenever she called home, Anya's grandmother would ask her if she had been to the beach yet, and each time she would make some excuse. Anya just wanted to bury herself in work. Because when she wasn't busy with the frenzy of the ER, her mind would be besieged by memories of Zoya. The very memories that Anya had hoped to escape from by moving to Goa. She wasn't doing a very good job of that though, she thought to herself. Now, at least, she would satisfy Beeji by telling her about her visit to the beach.

The small beach was emptying of visitors. The water had barely brushed against her feet when the whistle of the lifeguard alerted her to step back. She settled for a walk on the sand along the coastline, up to a small hillock a short distance away. When she returned to the point she had started from, the pattern of the clouds had changed. She didn't know what these ones were called, but she couldn't count on them not to pour. She decided to return to the campus. She could mark the beach visit on her checklist as 'done' and disappear into the labyrinths of the hospital again.

Back in her room, Anya arranged the groceries. She had been in Goa for more than a week, but she hadn't yet finished unpacking her things. She figured she would get the task out of the way. Her special frizzy hair shampoos went in the bathroom and her formal blouses at the back of her wardrobe. She kept her resistance bands in the dresser drawer and finally, she reached for the last object in the suitcase. The thought of unwrapping the brown paper wrapped package made her hands tremble. But she needed to know that the fragile snow globe that lay inside the bubble wrap had not been damaged during transit. She took a deep breath and began unwrapping it gingerly. She let the wrapping fall to the floor and gave the snow globe a fleeting glance to make sure it was intact. Spending more than a cursory moment looking at her favourite memento took a courage she would never find.

The long day and humid weather had taken its toll, and she felt a wave of tiredness. Despite that, sleep didn't come immediately—it no longer did, irrespective of how exhausted she was. After a while, she finally fell asleep. Meanwhile, the soft yellow light streaming in from the light posts outside gently fell on the snow globe containing the picture of Zoya and Anya at the London Eye; illuminating memories that would never fade from Anya's heart.

4

Sunrises and Smoothies

Roy was no stranger to sunrises. But, unlike this one, the many sunrises he had seen during his football practise days had been energising experiences. Right now, he could barely keep his eyes open as the rickety cab made its way to the H-of-H campus from the bus depot in Mapusa. What a miserable journey it had been.

Last week, he had travelled from Delhi to Bangalore for a cousin's wedding. The trip had been loads of fun; and the perfect way to chill before joining his new job at H-of-H. Everything had been perfect, except for the last leg of the holiday. On the way to the airport yesterday he had got a first-hand experience of the (in)famous Bangalore traffic. He still couldn't believe he had missed the last flight to Goa. He absolutely had to attend the induction program that started today. His new boss, who had already scheduled meetings in the next couple of days based on those sessions, would not take well to that. Roy had decided to take a flight to Mumbai and then figure out the rest. But nothing seemed to be happening without glitches. The airline misplacing his luggage had been the final flourish on his messed-up plans. Finally, after filling out baggage claim forms, he had taken the bus to Mapusa, where this tottering cab had been the only one available to take him to the hospital.

It couldn't have been a more chaotic start to life in a new city, a new job, and a new phase of his life.

The cab entered the H-of-H campus, and Roy referred to his email before following the signages for the Residences Block. Alighting, he didn't let his sullen mood provoke him to withhold a tip for the driver. Though the cab was rickety, the driver had been a good sort. He had even suggested quite a few options for grabbing a snack on the way, which Roy had refused.

"Hi! I am Dr Roy Bhaskar."

Roy went up to the sleepy gentleman at the reception, who wordlessly handed him the keys labelled 215.

"Need help with luggage?" he asked even though he showed no intention of moving from behind his desk.

"No, thanks. I don't have any."

There was no hint of surprise on the man's face on hearing this. "Does everyone lose their luggage when they come here?" Roy silently wondered.

The sparsely furnished studio apartment had a kitchenette with an induction hob and an attached bath. Roy quickly took out his laptop and chargers from his backpack and plugged in the gadgets. Fatigue and hunger were competing for his attention, but fatigue won. He took off his shoes and blazer and plonked himself on the bed. An hour later when his alarm rang, he was still groggy.

He splashed water on his face. He would have liked to shave the day-old stubble off, but his razor had been in his luggage too. He looked at his reflection in the mirror and sighed. His shirt was creased all over. His eyes looked as if he was having a hangover. He wore his blazer to hide the crumpled shirt, washed his eyes yet again and prayed for a source of caffeine so that he could last the entire day. The stubble, well, he was just going to have to wait to until he managed to find himself a new razor.

It was time for him to leave for the induction programme. He didn't know where the convention centre was and was sure that the gentleman at the reception wouldn't be a fountain of information. He better keep a time margin for finding his way—given how the last 24 hours had panned out, he would not be surprised if he got lost. He winced as he wore his shoes again and locked the door behind him.

"Hey, is there a general store around here?" Roy asked the only other person in the elevator with him.

"Hmm, there is one just outside the campus," Neel, who was going for his Sunday breakfast to Bordello's, replied.

"I don't think I have the time for that. I *need* to get to the convention centre."

"Can I help you with something? I am Neel."

"Hi, I am Roy. I just need to pick up some basic stuff. The airlines lost my luggage, and this stubble is making me look quite a ruffian."

"That should be easy to fix. I have a spare razor in my room. Why don't you come up with me so we can get it?"

"But you were heading out, right?"

"I can do that later."

As soon as Roy entered Neel's room, he took off his shoes and blazer. Every moment of comfort was worth savouring.

"Here you go. Instead of going back to your room, why don't you just use the washroom here?"

Roy hesitated, but Neel's suggestion did make sense.

As Roy freshened up, they talked about their work at H-of-H, and about Roy's travails in getting to Goa.

"That means you wouldn't have had breakfast!" Neel exclaimed.

"Err, yes, but that's okay. I will figure it out at the convention centre."

"I could fix you something while you freshen up."

"Hey, I don't want to put you to too much trouble. And I tend to be picky about food."

"It's no trouble at all. Milk and fruit work for you? And some toast of course?"

"Err. Just milk and fruit please."

When Roy emerged from the bathroom, Neel was pouring a smoothie into a tall glass.

Roy hesitated.

"Banana, apple, yogurt and some ice. That's what it takes to make a Sunday Special Smoothie." Neel announced with a smile.

Roy drained the smoothie. It was the best he had ever tasted.

"I could do with more of this."

Neel poured the remaining smoothie into Roy's glass.

"I think you just saved my life. I might have died of starvation if I hadn't bumped into you."

"Hey, you doctors are the ones who save lives. Lesser mortals like us work in accounts."

"Well, you just saved a life saver then. That is something."

Neel shrugged off the compliment.

"Have a good time. See ya later."

A FEW MONTHS AGO…

Roy loved the adrenaline rush that came with his job. The gratification of saving critical patients made being a trauma surgeon very rewarding. The Operating Room, a very intense and high stakes place, was where Roy was in his element. Even these days, after his breakup with Denise, when he was otherwise despondent and listless, he felt at home in the OR.

As he walked from the parking lot to the Level 1 Trauma Centre of the Neptune Hospital in Gurgaon where he worked, Roy hoped that his work would help him snap out of the melancholy. Yesterday evening had been particularly difficult. It would have been their 4th anniversary, and he had been unable to stop himself from wallowing in self-pity. It had been a relief when the restless night had turned to morning, and he could come in to work.

The wailing siren from the ambulance and the announcements from the building assailed his senses and he rushed. It was a car crash. Three college students had been driving up the highway when a lorry had crashed into them. Roy was allotted one of the patients, who had multiple internal injuries. After a quick examination, Roy decided that an emergency laparotomy (a procedure where they opened up the patient's abdomen and explored it completely to identify the organs injured and stop the bleeding) was needed. There was no time to lose, and Roy swung into action. In these cases, it was usually more than one organ that would be injured, and he methodically began to explore the abdominal cavity. A perforated gall bladder that he would need to remove was the first thing he noted. But before he did that, he needed to be sure that no other organ had been damaged, so he began to examine the intestine. A tear there could be fatal, and he needed to be sure he wasn't missing it. Suddenly, the patient's blood pressure dropped dangerously. In his hastiness, Roy panicked and accidently nicked the superior mesenteric artery. It was a potentially catastrophic mistake, and Roy was nonplussed. He just stood there, feeling the wetness of the rivulet of blood on his gloves, and watching gauze pieces exhaust their capacity for absorption. Until the other surgeon barked, "Roy, step back. I will be the lead now." Roy allowed his colleague to take his place in the team. The patient survived, though both the surgery and the post operative period would be longer and more complicated than they should have been.

The next few hours and days were tormenting. Roy revisited each moment of the surgery, especially the one when he had made that critical mistake. It was his fault. For the first time in his career, his concentration had wavered; that too at the most delicate moment. And this had happened because his breakup with Denise had been playing in his head. It was mortifying to confront the fact that he had risked his patient's life. His shame at how his inner world had affected his outer world was overwhelming. All that he could think of to quell the self-disgust was to go away somewhere, as far as possible. Maybe giving himself space would be good for him, he had thought. But whenever he checked out job descriptions and positions, the memory of blood gushing from where he had nicked the artery would spurt into his thoughts, plunging him into self-doubt. Finally, he signed up for a certificate course in hospital management. The short course was not as exciting as his days and nights in the OR, but becoming a student again after years kept him busy. And he had caught the attention of the course director Vijayant Naik. At the end of the course, Naik offered him a position in the administration of H-of-H.

"Just for a few months, Roy. Try it. You can leave whenever you like," Naik had said.

Before moving to Goa, Roy packed his schedule with activities with friends, family and reading up more on management. This façade of normalcy distracted him from the fear, which deep inside, was continuing to gnaw at him. Had the end of his relationship also meant the end of his confidence, and God forbid, his career as a surgeon too? He shuddered whenever the thought came up. By moving to Goa, he was pushing himself as far away from the unbearable thought as was possible.

5

Lucifer

The induction programme, mandatory for all doctors of H-of-H, was scheduled to begin in a short while.

Roy was taking in the panoramic view of the beach from the terrace of the convention centre. The Arabian Sea spread out ahead of him—its vast expanse both awing and beckoning him. He loved the ever-changing colours and moods of the ocean. After his eventful journey, he would have liked to have the day to himself and get out there on the seaside. But then he reminded himself, life rarely, if ever, worked out the way he wanted. He smiled the thought away, and sipped his coffee, which was too mild by his usual standards.

The coffee wasn't enough to put Anya in good spirits either. Having to wake up in the morning to listen to speeches was not her idea of fun. As far as she was concerned, these fancy 'induction processes' and 'relationship building' were part of the corporate culture that had seeped into medicine. Never in her training had she needed more than basic perfunctory introductions before plunging headfirst into work. For her, looking after patients was the most important relationship of all. But attendance was mandatory, and here she was, wasting a perfectly good day.

She added her usual two spoons of sugar into her coffee and stirred it. She had developed quite a liking for poee—the traditional Goan bread and picked up a slice.

The first session was about the growth plans of the hospital, but Anya didn't really care. If there was one thing that the last year had taught her, it was that there was no point in making any plans. Life would attack those plans with an unimaginable vengeance. She tuned out the presentations and doodled on her notepad.

Roy, sitting in the front, was listening intently and taking notes. He knew Vijayant would quiz him about the presentation.

Finally, the sessions came to an end, and it was time for lunch.

Anya rushed to the pasta counter and requested the chef for fusilli in red sauce and a generous dollop of cream.

"Only some grilled vegetables please. No pasta," Roy was already there, placing his request.

Weird. Who goes to a pasta counter, and doesn't want pasta? And who wears a blazer in the sweltering June heat of Goa? Anya thought.

A little while later, Roy was just ahead of her in the buffet queue. He curiously examined each item at the salad counter, then paused before taking teeny bits of the cucumber and raw papaya salad. *If he didn't want to eat them, why was he looking at them?* Anya was annoyed. He was taking forever; and standing behind him left her having to choose between staring at his shoulders or the floor. Once she was done noting his brown mop of hair that faded into a taper at the neckline and the mole behind his left ear, she took in those fancy brown shoes, tapered at the toes. *Might as well play the guessing game while he looks at the spread of food like a forlorn lover,* she thought. She checked off the boxes in her head as she inched along behind him. Maybe he was from the housekeeping services—no; facility management was the correct term given his blazer and fancy shoes. Pointy shoes could mean administration or marketing. He must be one of those guys who had all the time in the world to create 360-degree questionnaires, which she hated so much.

Waiting had made her hungrier. She filled up on rice, chicken, fish, and the mixed vegetables at one go. She couldn't risk getting stuck behind him again. Once done, she headed towards the dessert counter. It was a relief to find Pointy-Shoes nowhere near the desert counter. Of course, someone who ate only salads wouldn't want to eat dessert. Must be a fitness freak type. The lemon soufflé was delicious and she picked up a second helping.

The screen announced, 'Team Building'. Such corporate style kitsch was enough to ruffle Anya's feathers. If this had been an online event, her fingers wouldn't have moved from the eye roll emoji.

"Let us all introduce ourselves."

In a flash, Pointy-Shoes was on the stage.

"I am Roy Bhaskar. I am a surgeon. But, here I will be working with Dr Naik in hospital management."

"Dr Anya Chopra. Emergency physician," she kept her introduction brief.

She checked her messages as she waited for the rest of the introductions to finish. There was a text from Neel: "How is it going? Want to meet for table tennis later?"

In Goa, Anya had found a comforting presence in Neel. The meeting over pakoras had been the start of a gentle, amiable friendship. Without her realising it, Neel had been able to bring her out of the cocoon of aloofness she had been weaving around herself. She looked forward to their usual games of table tennis and walks to Pedro's. Neel, the quintessential dreamer, reminded her of Zoya. Especially his love for clouds, which was a throwback to her sister's fascination for the stars. Both found meaning—and comfort—in the abstract and the intangible. Anya found it endearing.

She typed back: "There is a banquet after the session. Maybe tomorrow?"

In between presentations Roy quickly checked his messages. There was nothing of any importance; instead,

6

Jenga and Bagels

Anya was in the common room, waiting for Neel. They had planned to go for coffee, but he was running late. When Roy walked in, he found Anya texting furiously and scowling at the phone, muttering to herself. He recognised Anya—those scowls had been hard to miss on the day of the induction programme.

He waved at her in acknowledgement and opened his laptop. Anya waved back and continued texting. She didn't want to miss out on the free bagels that the café was offering today. If Neel didn't reply in a few minutes, she would have to go alone. As she waited, she looked at Roy who was busy on his laptop. *Like some corporate honcho*, Anya thought, disdainfully.

Even though she had hardly interacted with Roy, Anya had heard enough chatter in the hospital about the new hospital manager. Anya understood that Roy was Naik's protégée but she still found it odd that he had chosen to work in management rather than surgery.

Roy finished with the emails for meetings about the new maternity wing and shut his laptop. Naik had been right about H-of-H being a good place to work, he mused. The common room had a foosball table, table tennis, a

there was a notification from Google Photos. It was a picture of Denise and Roy in their favourite café where they shared bubble tea, jokes and dreams of a future together.

He quickly put away his phone. He didn't want any reminder of how quickly his texts to Denise had transformed to long telephone chats and dates. It was almost a year since the breakup, but the pain still felt fresh. He never wanted to feel that kind of pain again.

By the time the sessions ended, it was evening.

Roy hurried to the Residences Block. The event had been mind-numbingly boring. And, thanks to his missing luggage, he had had to literally sweat it out in his blazer. The shoes were terribly uncomfortable too. And then, there had been this emergency physician whose eyes he could feel boring into his back in the lunch break. She had been so restless and impatient in the queue. He shrugged his irritation off.

He really needed to go into the city to buy himself a change of clothes and comfortable loafers.

"Hi! Any idea where I can rent a bike?" Roy pinged Neel, who replied by sharing Pedro's contact.

Dinner was simple and informal. Pointy-Shoes was not around. Anya enjoyed Dr Rodrigues' company, especially the anecdotes from his long career. Instead of starting with the patients' symptoms or diagnosis, he always told them about the person that the patient was. Who they were, what they did, even what they liked—things that were unrelated to their doctor's visits. Dr Malathi Kini regaled them with a soft, lilting traditional Konkani song. A little before midnight, Anya returned to her room tired—and just a little tipsy from the rum that Rodrigues had convinced her to try. She texted Neel. "Dr Rodrigues has so many interesting stories to share!"

"Yeah! He is quite cool!" Neel replied immediately.

For Neel too, the friendship with Anya had been an instant camaraderie. Anya didn't question his quirk for watching clouds. He didn't feel as if she was judging him or comparing him to the usual yardsticks many others did. She hadn't asked him any of the tiresome questions—'Both your parents are doctors; how come you didn't choose a career in medicine? Why do you keep switching jobs?'

"How was dinner?" he texted back.

She replied with the martini and lip smacking emojis.

In his apartment, Roy was finally in comfortable clothes. He dropped ice cubes in the blender and whirred his iced latte. His coffees could give many a café a good run for their money. The latte and the message from the airlines saying his luggage would reach tomorrow made him feel better. The rotisserie grilled chicken he had picked up

on his way back wasn't great, but he was famished finished it at one go. Then he tuned into *Lucifer*.

Meanwhile, the rum had a paradoxical effect on A and left her feeling wide awake. She decided to v *Lucifer*.

reading nook, a large TV and a carpeted area for board games. It had been raining almost every day since he had arrived, and he hadn't been able to check out Goa's famous football clubs yet. The foosball table would be a less than satisfactory substitute, but it would be fun. He took his place along one side of the table and began manoeuvring the rods.

"Need company?" Anya called out to him.

"Sure."

Anya was as good a player as he was. She had a very strong defence. They played in a silence which was charged with the air of competition.

The score was tied at 2-2 when Neel walked in.

"Hey. I thought we would have to give up on the free bagels."Anya said as soon as he entered.

Neel grinned. "I would never have heard the end of it if that happened, would I?"

"Hey Roy, how have you been?"

"All good."

"Join us? We are going out for a coffee. It's free bagel day."

"Hmm, really not sure about that." Roy said.

"Please decide quickly. They run out of those fabulous bagels by evening." Anya almost snapped.

She was already walking towards the door. Neel beckoned him. "Come with us."

The three of them walked out of the hospital gates and went to the cafe, where only a few tables were vacant.

Anya and Neel chewed on the bagels as they sipped their Americanos. Roy, who had asked for a flat white, didn't touch his bagel even when Anya prompted him. "Don't waste a freebie."

"Err, I avoid bakes. You can have it if you like."

"Of course, you are a salad type." Anya grinned.

Roy didn't like the jibe but decided to let it go.

It was Neel and Anya who did most of the talking. Roy was mostly silent, watching the Formula 1 telecast on the TV that occupied one wall of the café. By the time the race and the bagels were over, it had begun to pour outside. Roy began stacking the Jenga blocks in the usual set of threes. "Anyone in for a game of Jenga?"

"Yeah!" Neel replied.

They waited for Anya who was checking the weather status on her phone.

"Anya, we don't need Accuweather to tell us it's raining outside." Neel called out with a smile.

"Ok, might well as play Jenga. We wouldn't have been stuck if you had come on time." Anya rebutted, but with a smile. That was the thing with Neel—he had this tenderness which ensured that you couldn't stay mad at him for long. With him, the usually oversensitive Anya managed to take things in the right spirit.

She joined them on the floor for Jenga. Roy wondered if she would be as impatient and fidgety as she had been in the buffet queue the other day.

Neel was good at the game, Anya not so much. As Zoya had always said, it was Anya's impatience that got in the way in things. She would be in a hurry to take her turn or she would lose her patience while withdrawing the block.

Anya was the first to be eliminated. Roy and Neel continued, giving each other stiff competition. Anya watched with bated breath, expecting the tower to collapse when Roy, his eyebrows knitted closely in deep concentration, opted for a tough move. With a steady hand, he reached for a wooden block in the middle zone of the tower. Despite the precariousness of the move, the tower remained standing. Anya and Neel were discovering that Roy was the undisputed Jenga champion.

Roy enjoyed Jenga. Both playing and winning it. His first memories were of playing the game to pass the incessant hours he spent in hospitals as a young child. It was a good distraction from the injections and scans. Later in life, he had rediscovered Jenga as a tool to build his concentration. Focussing on the tower of blocks taught him to shut himself to the noise and clutter outside. Removing those blocks and replacing them was an act of skill, judgement, clarity of thought and confidence—all of which were critical in medicine, even more so to a trauma surgeon. They had also been qualities he had needed to nurture in his football playing days. Days which he hoped to relive at least a bit in Goa, which had a notable football culture.

By the time they finished with their game of Jenga, the rain had abated somewhat, but they decided to wait for it to completely stop before leaving. Neel was in the kitchen befriending the owner, Dinah. Roy was checking emails on his laptop, and Anya was becoming restless. She began watching the political debate that was running on the TV.

The running captions on the TV screen were flashing international news. An assault on a place of worship that was possibly a hate crime in London was being covered. Suddenly Anya felt the world closing in on her. Her heart was pounding fast. It was as if she was having a nightmare, but a part of her knew that she was awake. It was a strange visceral experience that lasted only a few seconds, but felt as if it was much longer. In those few seconds, it was as if the phone call that had informed her family of Zoya's death was happening again. She could hear the phone ring and a heavily accented voice speak those words which had changed her life forever.

The captions changed and Anya's breathing settled. But she was drained by the episode which she herself couldn't understand. This had never happened to her before.

Roy had noticed that something was wrong. He observed the distant glazed look in her eyes, and her pale face. He wondered what the matter was but wasn't sure if he should ask.

"Would you like some water?" he asked her.

"Yes, thanks."

Anya sipped the water slowly. She was overwhelmed. She could feel her face flush with embarrassment. Roy would have found her behaviour strange.

"I am not sure what happened…" Anya could feel tears waiting to gush out.

Roy sensed that her composure was fragile. He let her sit in silence, not prodding her for information, nor offering platitudes.

"I am sorry, I don't know what happened."

"Don't be sorry, Anya. It's okay." The kindness in Roy's voice took away Anya's discomfiture. Later into their friendship she would discover that this kindness was rooted in pain. Right now, she relaxed a little.

After a while, the rain had stopped. Neel had also returned from the kitchen with baking tips.

As they walked back, Neel told them about the low-lying fluffy clouds that rain usually leaves behind.

Anya was still confused—and a little self-conscious—after what had happened in the café. Roy walked silently beside her, not forcing her to make conversation.

They had almost reached the hospital gate when Anya whispered, "Zoya". Roy slowed down to match her pace. He could tell that this was very difficult for her.

"My sister…Zoya. She was killed in a hate crime in the USA. I think the TV triggered memories…"

Anya's voice faltered.

Neel took Anya's hand in his.

"So sorry to hear that. This must have been so difficult for you." Roy's voice was gentle, kind, warm and caring. They walked back in silence.

Back in her apartment, Anya took a double dose of sedatives and hoped for sleep to come and rescue her from the memories.

7

Friendship

The trio soon developed a routine of hanging out together. Jenga, foosball, table tennis and walks to Pedro's were how they spent much of their spare time. The beach, of course, was their favourite place. Roy collecting seashells, Anya sharing the latest music from her playlist and Neel watching clouds—their favourite pastimes quickly became woven into their evening beach outings.

Anya and Roy often spoke about the hospital, patients or their rigorous training days. The conversations didn't leave Neel with the familiar discomfort that dining table conversations back home did. His friends didn't make their profession seem like child's play. They talked of their triumphs and wins but also of doubts, of misdiagnoses, of fears and even mistakes; of the flawed, struggling people in their workplaces who worked together in high-stakes situations. Anya and Roy weren't like the unbelievably infallible doctors who streamed on television shows—which is how he had always imagined his parents to be. Neel would explain cloud formations to his friends, dropping names like Cirrostratus and Stratocumulus as easily as they dropped Choledocholithiasis, Marfan's syndrome or Pneumoconiosis. Roy and Anya would stare at the clouds trying—often unsuccessfully—to see the configurations that Neel found effortlessly in them.

Anya would mostly avoid talking about Zoya, but her friends understood the impact that the tragedy had had on her. When Anya and Neel would look up restaurants to check out on the internet, Roy would fall silent; and they would keep scanning the menus until Roy found something that was agreeable to him. Neel would not speak about the many jobs and hobbies he had switched, and Anya and Roy didn't bring up Neel's famous parents.

A close comfort zone quickly developed between the trio. Their WhatsApp group became their lifeline. Within a few weeks, they were hanging out every evening catching up in the hospital cafeteria whenever they could and of course, checking out the Chapora Fort (a la *Dil Chahta Hai*) on their rented motorcycles. They would make plans to explore Goa, discuss offbeat places and things to try out in the city they had come to in search of an escape.

All of them had been struggling with their own demons before coming to Goa and hadn't expected to find a kinship like they did in this nascent friendship. A lot of what weighed them down remained unspoken, yet, they felt lighter. It was as if they had been lonely night travellers on a long arduous journey. Now, even though they couldn't see the light yet, the darkness had shifted a little. Enough to be able to see the road immediately ahead of them. And, as it often does, that was what made a huge difference.

8

Fleeting Joys

Roy looked at the calendar on his laptop. Choc-a-bloc with annotations of different colours, it signalled another busy day. Naik had given Roy the responsibility of getting the maternity wing, which was already running behind schedule, completed as soon as possible. Roy always found packed schedules invigorating. But here, in Goa, the agenda was meetings, not surgical procedures; and he was not enthused. The energy and action of the OR was far removed from the dreary discussions in conference rooms. He missed that terribly. But he didn't have the confidence to venture into the OR again. What if he goofed up again?

The opportunity to join H-of-H had presented itself when he had been at the lowest ebbs of despair. And also, shame. Breaking up with Denise had been extremely painful. It wasn't just the ending of the relationship that had left him numb, it was how Denise accused him of being selfish and self-centred. *"Everything always revolves around you. Where we go. What we do. What we eat. It's all about you, Roy!"*

"You are so high maintenance. It's such a pain being with you."

"Don't you think it's time you gave up on your obsession with football?"

It was ironical how she had caustically added 'Grow up'. After all, much of his childhood had been spent in illness, forcing him to be mature beyond his years.

So far, Goa hadn't been bad. In the little time that he managed to steal from work, he would rush to the football grounds.

He and Neel had become good friends, and Anya wasn't too bad either. After their initial interactions at the hospital orientation, which hadn't gone off too well, things had somewhat settled. He enjoyed the evenings or days off when they hung out together. He noted that she was rather silent on their walks. But in a game, she was usually spirited—and competitive; and he enjoyed the keen contest that they invariably had in foosball.

But, in spite of all this, there was a discontent inside him that refused to be quelled.

Roy looked at the agenda for the day. He sighed as he noted that he had to meet with the maintenance wing, the fire safety department and the marketing team. Not much of medicine that he was doing, was he? He reminded himself that even though management wasn't as fulfilling as surgery, the packed schedule was keeping him occupied, and not giving him much opportunity to think about the applications for the polytrauma fellowship which would open soon. Or from the reasons for his being here, wearing blazers and formal shoes instead of scrubs, as Anya would put it. Though no one in Goa, not even his new friends, knew about the episode which had dented his confidence so severely, the events were seldom far from his own thoughts. They seemed to accompany him everywhere. Even in the most sacrosanct of places—the OR. Would that ever stop?

Not long ago, he had desperately wanted to train in polytrauma. But now he hesitated to even fill in the applications. Maybe he didn't have it in him anymore? Maybe, like football, surgery was also a dream that was destined to be short lived, a fleeting phase of happiness that he must now learn to live without?

9

Mist and Clouds

Neel and Roy were immersed in a game of Scotland Yard. Neel easily trumped them both when it came to board games. Anya was checking out Dudhsagar Falls on Trip Advisor.

"Are we on for Sunday?" she asked.

"Yeah!"

"I want to be there in the afternoon to catch a glimpse of the train passing through the falls," Roy said.

"Yes, that will be great. Let's also ask Pedro for tips," Neel said.

They put away the game and walked towards Pedro's.

"Hey Pedro, we are planning a trip to Dudhsagar Falls. Any thoughts?" Anya asked while Neel went straight inside where Grace was stocking the shelves.

"Yes, be careful of the mosquitoes. And you must make a video of the water falling from the height. It is one of the most spectacular sights ever seen." Anya never failed to be impressed by Pedro's zest for life despite his disability.

After chatting briefly with Pedro, Anya and Roy went inside to find Grace and Neel immersed in an intense discussion. Grace would soon be turning entrepreneur with her restaurant. When she had been stuck with the forms and paperwork, Roy had pulled a few strings through Dr Naik. Neel had also offered to help her set up operations.

"The permit for the restaurant has come through. Thank you, Dr Roy, for your help."

"Anytime, Grace. So, is Neel helping you with the billing software and accounts?"

"Actually, we have been planning the menu." Grace replied enthusiastically.

Neel looked up from the bundle of recipe books, a satisfied grin on his face.

"Since most of the eateries in this area are shacks with a mixed cuisine menu, I think we should offer mostly traditional Goan recipes. Those will be our USP—though they will need to be customised for universal acceptance."

Roy and Anya exchanged smiles. Their friend, who usually had his head in the clouds, was always grounded and present whenever food was in the picture. He had a flair for the nuances of food—cooking it, analysing it, even plating it.

They alighted from the jeep for the last stretch which was a 5 km long trek. Anya noted Roy's concentration and confidence as he navigated the steep parts. It wasn't that she herself found them difficult, but Roy's sure-footed steps on the *kuccha* road made Anya realise that his was a different level of mental and physical fitness—the kind that sportspersons had. And leaders too. Roy was a natural and was thoroughly in his element.

Roy waited at a curve for them to join him. He had been surprised at how quickly Anya had got the hang of the trek. But then, as he had come to understand, Anya loved a challenge. Every opportunity to prove her mettle brought out the best in her. That was something they had in common.

Anya joined him in a few moments. They watched as Neel took his time, dawdling as usual, lost in his thoughts and enjoying the floating wispy clouds in the clear blue sky.

The tiered falls, in their post rainfall glory, were awe inspiring. The height from which the water cascaded into the gorge below gave it a unique sound—forceful and almost angry, which was very different from the soft crashing of the waves on to the seashore that they now enjoyed every day.

"Isn't this magnificent?" Anya was mesmerised.

"Yes, it is." Neel, who had caught up with them, agreed.

"We should have trekked the entire way, along the railway track, from Castle Rock." Roy said.

"Yes, Roy, but that needs the entire day. And you have tele-cons lined up—even on a Sunday evening!" Neel chided.

"True." Roy now had the additional charge of the accreditation process of the hospital, and he was keeping himself on a strict timeline.

The trio sat on one of the rocks, feeling the freshness of the light shower of water on their faces.

Neel reached for his backpack and pulled out the lunch boxes he had offered to pack for the outing.

"Neel, these cream cheese sandwiches are fabulous."

"Thanks, Anya. Hey, Roy, dig into this salad."

Roy looked at his friend in amazement. Neel could elevate even a rough-it-out outing into a gourmet experience. The guy had serious talent. And he consistently refused to acknowledge it or do something about it.

"Neel, why are you not in the food business?" Roy asked.

Neel looked embarrassed.

"Food business? Is that even a thing?"

On a single occasion, when he was a college fresher, Neel had told his father about his interest in cooking and in food. This is what his father had said then. Even though that had been a decade ago, Neel had clung onto those words. He had repeated them a million times to himself since then and had started believing them to be true. Never mind that almost a decade had passed since then, that his passion for food had only increased, or that he had not brought up a possibility of a career in the food business to his parents since then.

Roy looked at him incredulously. "It's not just a thing. It's a huge thing. And you are the perfect person for it."

"Neel, come here. Have you seen the mist from the waterfalls here? I can't tell if its clouds or water." Anya beckoned Neel.

"Anya, clouds *are* water." Neel grinned. He had understood what she meant, but couldn't pass up an occasion to pull Anya's leg.

She was right though. It was a spectacular view. But even as he took it in, the conversation that he had just been having with Roy lingered in his mind.

"Look, do you see it?" This time it was Roy asking for Neel's attention.

"What? Where?"

"A rainbow."

Neel looked in the direction that Roy had indicated and there it was—a fragile, tenuous band of colour, barely visible through the mist.

The three adults stood enthralled by the serendipitous finding for a while, as if they were children taking in its magic. For a few moments, maybe they were.

10

A Lacerated Spleen

The ER was unusually busy. Anya had just finished stitching a nasty forehead wound when the next patient arrived.

"Twenty-five-year-old female with dizziness that won't go away. Vitals are stable." The paramedic screamed.

She went towards the patient bay, narrowing down the possibilities in her head. It could be nothing, or it could be life threatening. The patient, a healthy-looking young woman, was reasonably calm. The pulse and breathing were normal too.

"Would you like to tell me what's wrong?"

"Doctor, I am feeling lightheaded. Weak and woozy."

The paramedic had hooked up a monitor and was drawing a blood sample. The blood pressure was normal too. Maybe the lab work would show anaemia.

"When did you have your last meal, Tess?"

"I had breakfast at around 8. Then I climbed up on the kitchen counter to pick up one of the large jars on the top of the cabinet and I slipped and fell. But I didn't hurt myself. So, I got dressed for college, where I teach. On the way, I felt lightheaded—as if I might lose control of my scooter, so I came here instead."

"You fell from the kitchen counter?"

"Yes, but I didn't hurt myself. The corner of the kitchen slab broke my fall. It wasn't a big deal."

Tess winced as she shifted from the chair to the bed. Anya noticed the small but significant dip in blood pressure when that happened. She increased the flow of IV fluid and began the abdominal examination. Only a slight wince, that too on deep palpation. By itself, it probably meant nothing, but coupled with the history of the fall and the drop in BP, it was something that Anya wasn't going to ignore.

"Can you page Radiology for an urgent ultrasound?" Anya called out to the nursing officer.

"What happened, doctor?" Tess looked worried.

"Just having everything checked out for you. Could you be pregnant?"

"No, doctor. I had a miscarriage about a fortnight ago. Maybe it's that weakness returning."

"Could be. Let's check out all possibilities."

"Pelvis Ultrasound please, to check for retained products of conception." She requested the radiologist, who quickly began her scan.

"The uterus and adnexa are normal."

Anya went back to Tess and asked her to lie on her left side, and pressed deep into her abdomen.

"Ouch."

The BP dropped again.

"Let me check the upper abdomen too."

Anya stepped back and waited for the scan to be completed.

"Hmm, there is a tiny collection of fluid." The radiologist remarked. "It's small but is obscuring the spleen." Her tone changed. "Or maybe, it *is* the spleen…"

Anya understood what the radiologist meant.

"This could be a splenic injury. Need a surgical consult stat. And an urgent abdominal CT." Anya shouted towards the nurse's station.

A few minutes later, she heard a deep—and familiar voice—ask, "Non penetrating trauma to abdomen, right?" It was Roy.

"Yes. I have asked for a CT scan." Anya looked up from her notes and continued, "But what are you doing here?"

"The surgical team is handling a double kidney transplant. I am covering for them," Roy replied.

He deftly folded the legs of the patient at the knee and gently examined her, dictating his notes to Miriam as he did so. Then, he addressed Tess, "There could be an injury to your spleen, which we will confirm by a CT scan. If we don't operate immediately, it will not stop bleeding. We will need to remove the spleen." Roy spoke gently but firmly, blending confidence and compassion.

Anya watched as he continued to speak with Tess. Despite the urgency with which he was writing out the instructions, Roy managed to give his patient his complete attention. She was impressed with his bedside manner.

Roy called for the ER manager. "Please have the patient prepped for surgery. I will meanwhile page the surgical team; they will need to spare two surgeons for this."

Just a few moments later, Anya noticed Roy at the monitoring station in the centre of the ER. He was looking visibly tense.

"Hey, the patient is stable, isn't she?"

"Yes," he replied tersely. "At least for now."

Anya knew that this was true. An internal bleed was a very unpredictable situation, and there was always a chance of a patient decompensating. But, they had stabilised her and the surgery would be starting soon. All bases were covered. Then why was Roy nibbling at his fingernails and pacing?

"What's the problem?"

"The double transplant had a complication. The surgeons are caught up there, and it may be a while before they can get out of that."

"So what? Ask them for a resident to assist you?"

"Assist *me*?"

"Yes, of course. Why wait for them, when you are a trauma surgeon?"

Anya scurried off to see a new patient, even as Roy stared silently at the telephone he had put down a few moments ago.

Roy's silence belied the tempestuous storm within him. He had not operated since that episode, which had been uncannily similar to this patient. A young patient with abdominal trauma. It was unnerving. There was no way he could put himself in a similar situation again. But waiting could be fatal for Tess.

The shrill sound of the telephone wasn't enough to break his rumination. It was the OR manager who had to tap him on his shoulder.

"Dr Naik…for you."

The receiver felt cold in Roy's clammy, sweaty hands.

Naik, as usual, didn't waste time on pleasantries.

"Roy, you are going to have to take up the splenic laceration. I have asked for OR 4 to be reserved for you. I will send a resident and an OR technician. Do you need anyone else on your team?'"

Try as he might, Roy was unable to say anything. Not that there was anything that he could have said. There was really nothing complicated in this surgery—not for someone with his experience. He had done many similar procedures. But those had all been before that fateful day, which had become a watershed event in his life.

The phone went dead.

Anya returned to find Roy still lost in his thoughts. Except that now he wasn't pacing; he was still. He was exuding tension from each pore of his body—

definitely not the best state of mind to perform a critical intervention.

"What happened?"

"Anya, it has been so long since I operated."

How could he tell Anya the events in the OR that day which still haunted him?

Anya sensed that he was struggling but didn't know what was bothering him. What she did know was that overthinking was not what an emergency situation demanded. She believed that when Roy overcame his hesitation and swung into action, his training and experience would take over and he would find himself in his element as a surgeon. She took his hand in hers.

"So what, Roy? You have been a surgeon for so many years. You have so much experience. Isn't being a doctor like learning swimming or cycling; doesn't it become a party of your body, mind and soul? You can't forget or unlearn what you have learnt." Then, softly, she added, "You've got this, Roy. It's going to be okay."

She wasn't sure how much of her words had penetrated the cloud of doubt that Roy had cloaked himself in. She could just hope it was enough. She went back to check on Tess, whose vitals remained stable.

Despite Roy's paralysing fears, Anya's words had found their mark. Was she right, he wondered? A few years ago—before Denise, that is—this case would have got the adrenaline pumping and he would have rushed to the OR. Now, his heart was racing, but out of fear rather than the anticipation of a challenge. This wouldn't do. Not at all. Especially since Tess's life depended on it.

Roy took a deep breath and shut his eyes for a moment. He hoped visualisation, something his therapist had introduced him to, would work. He imagined himself—not in the OR but on the football field, his eyes fixated on the ball. For the next couple of hours, nothing except the patient and the procedure would matter. He needed to be that Roy again. He owed it to the patient, even more than he owed it to himself.

It had taken a while, but the moments of doubt were fading away, and self-assurance had built up.

Roy turned to the nursing officer.

"Please get the lab reports and have the patient shifted."

The instructions were brisk and taut—the kind that comes from a person who is totally in control.

Then Roy went up to Anya.

"I am short of assistants. The resident on call is scrubbing, but I will need one more doctor as a backup."

"I could glove up... My shift here is almost over."

"Perfect. See you in the OR."

Anya watched him sweep out of the ER, his movements brisk, fluid, and precise. She was suddenly curious. If this was a preview of Roy in the OR, the real performance would be interesting.

11

The Surgery

Anya loved the OR too. Choosing between Surgery and Emergency Medicine had been a tough call for her. She found the thrill of piecing together clues to make a diagnosis as interesting as solving a mystery; and this had tilted the scales in favour of her becoming an emergency physician. Still, she would sometimes feel nostalgic for the air of anticipation and dramatic vibe in the OR. The luminescent lights, glistening metal instruments in gleaming sterile trays and the rows of equipment made the OR a unique experience. Many of her teachers had used the term 'Operation Theatre' for the OR. It did seem more appropriate given how the place was a stage for the most difficult procedures. After all, each case was a performance, a symphony of actions of so many people, events, and things. No matter how many rehearsals were done, it was the moment of truth when the patient was wheeled in. And there was no scope for retakes, edits, touch ups, or computerised imagery. It was as real as it could get.

She began to scrub.

Inside the OR, Roy was sitting on a rotating stool in the corner, already scrubbed and gloved. He was again imagining himself on the football field; this time preparing for the clincher penalty shot. The crowd was cheering loudly, but the sound faded out. He saw only the ball and focussed on the goal post. That was the similarity between football and surgery. Both had an urgency about them and needed quick action. But the paradox was that the action could have the desired impact only if it had its roots in practise, analysis and strategising. What happened on the fields—and on the operating table—was a result of all that had been internalised during hours of practise. On the field, it had been just him and the ball. Here, it was just him and the patient. Nothing else counted. Time, tasks, thirst, troubles—all had to be left behind. Surgery demanded concentration and observation so intense that he could pick up warning signals from a silent patient; that he could be alerted to creating innovative solutions if they were needed. Each patient demanded—and deserved—perfection; mediocrity was not an option. The performance needed to be flawless. On the operating table, the scalpel needed to make a bold, unwavering, confident incision. And today—after months—he would be making that incision. He took a deep breath and surrendered himself to the only one that mattered in that moment—his young patient.

As the OR became abuzz with activity and the patient was wheeled in, Roy felt good to be in scrubs again. Maybe he could wear scrubs to work on days he didn't have meetings, or at least get rid of those formal shoes that seemed to be designed for people who had had three toes amputated. Or he could offer to cover for the surgery team more often—something that he had avoided whenever Naik suggested it.

He made the incision sliced through the layers of skin, fascia and muscle.

Anya's eyes followed the scalpel, then his hands and his arms.

Anya saw how he was deeply focussed. He seemed oblivious to the low, constant noise of people speaking, equipment whirring, and monitors beeping. Just like Zoya, when she would be handling a complicated pregnancy. Or when Anya herself would be intubating a patient. This was the real Roy, doing what he really loved. She watched him use the suction to clear the cavity of the blood.

She couldn't help it when her eyes rested on the part of his chest that remained exposed in the scrubs, the sinewy hair standing out in the golden yellow beam of light from the overhead operating lamp.

"Anya, this is where I will need your help. Can you please hold this retractor for me? Firmly, but without too much pressure."

She shifted her attention from the surgeon to the surgery.

His field of vision clear, Roy finally saw the spleen. It was turgid with the blood. He identified the injury and the offender vessel which was oozing a few millilitres at a time. A grade 1 laceration. He quizzed the surgical resident who had joined them about the classification of splenic injuries. And he wondered if he had been wrong about his decision to remove the spleen. For a surgeon, humility and arrogance went hand in hand. If the blunt arrogance that nothing would go wrong was essential; so was the humility to recognise that they may need to revise and review their decisions. Fixing the bleed was possible, but it was a more complicated task. In an earlier life, he would have revised his plan immediately. Now, he vacillated, but just for a moment. The best possible thing for the patient was repair not removal. And each patient deserved the best option.

He took a deep, long breath.

Anya watched as the trainee listened and observed in rapt attention. There was no doubt about it. Roy was a star in the OR. A surgeon was the leader of a huge interdisciplinary team, and Roy was a natural. What was he doing pushing files? Why was he wasting his life and throwing away a stellar career?

"I don't think we need to do a splenectomy. I can fix the bleed." Roy's voice filled the OR. She could feel a stillness crop up around her—everyone was taking in Roy's words. The team realised that this was a critical decision. One that was a test of both the skill and clinical judgement of the surgeon. Not every surgeon would be able to take the decision with so much confidence. But Roy's self-assured stance dissolved any doubts they might have had.

"Repairing a splenic rupture is a tedious, more complex process. But where it is possible, we must try a conservative approach." Roy addressed the surgical resident, who clearly hadn't seen this coming. Roy answered the unasked question, "Yes, it is a judgement call. But then, everything in life is one, isn't it? In surgery, as in life, you must have the spine to make difficult calls and follow them through."

Again, Anya watched his hands. Deft, nimble, and precise. He sutured the bleed carefully. Then he double checked the repair and proceeded to close, while documenting the procedure on a voice note.

They filed out to the anteroom. The feeling after a surgery—when the cast returns from the stage to the wings—is also unique. The tension has dissipated, the guard can be lowered, and the coffee can be savoured. Sweet buns were passed around, and Anya took two.

Roy dictated the post-op instructions. He was hungry too, but he let the buns pass. He looked at Anya. The high ponytail and frizzy opinionated hair were finally out of the surgical cap and falling over her face. She was devouring the buns and had put her feet up on the single footstool in the room—as if she had been the lead surgeon and was exhausted after a major surgery. He smiled. It had been good having her around.

"I need to get back to my office for some calls. Would you do me a favour and check on Tess later?" Roy asked Anya.

"Sure."

Roy returned to his room and reached into his drawer for an energy bar.

Anya lingered on, waiting for the patient to be shifted to post-op. Being part of an Operating Team after so many years had been exhilarating. And watching Roy operate had been like watching poetry in motion. In all the time they hung out together, he hardly spoke about his training and work in surgery, but it was obvious that he was very accomplished. She checked out Roy's LinkedIn profile. A trauma surgeon with a fellowship in abdominal trauma; and one of the few Indian doctors to have received the 'Silver Scalpel' award for upcoming surgeons. A very impressive profile indeed. She would never have known it from the single line introduction on the H-of-H app which simply stated, '*Roy is a surgeon and hospital manager.*'

Like the ocean that he loved, Roy hid a lot beneath his surface. He had so many layers to him, and it felt as if she could never completely get to know him. *Why did he keep his real self hidden even from his friends?*

12

Acute Abdomen

Anya had finished with her morning shift. She decided to check if Roy was free for coffee.

She knocked on Roy's door, but there was no reply. He was spending a lot of his time in the maternity wing these days, and she decided to use his intercom to call and check over there.

The first thing she saw when she entered his office was the glass jar on the desk. It was full of seashells—of different colours, glistening and reflecting the light, and with patterns and shapes varying from whorls, spirals and conches. So, this was where he kept all those seashells he collected from their walks on the beach.

Only when she reached for the telephone on his desk, did she notice Roy in the sofa on the corner, doubled up and quivering in pain. His eyes were sunken in his face, and he could hardly speak. Beads of perspiration were forming on his forehead despite the air conditioning.

"Roy!" She took in his pale face and examined his pulse, it was fast but regular. Then she reached for the stethoscope around her neck.

"I don't need that, Anya."

"Of course, you do. And an ECG too. I need to be sure you are not having an MI."

"It's not my heart."

Roy managed to get the words out before another wave of pain stabbed at his stomach.

"How come you always know everything? We need to get you to the ER."

"Anya, listen to me. It's my stomach."

"Okay. Let us get an X-Ray. Need to rule out obstruction."

"It's not an obstruction."

"How do you know, Roy? You need to let others manage a situation for once."

It was a jibe, but not the caustic one that she sometimes directed at him. It was tender and filled with concern.

A spike of severe pain shot through him, and he clutched at Anya's hand.

She had never him seen him so vulnerable.

"Anya, there is an injectable cartridge in my desk drawer. Please get me that."

"What is it?"

"Anya. Just do it. Let me be the doctor please."

"I think we should get you to the ER."

"Anya, listen. I have a complicated set of food allergies since childhood. That is why I am very careful about what I eat. I don't know what triggered it this time."

He was shivering.

She opened the drawer and found the cartridge.

"Do you want me to inject it, or do you want to continue being the doctor?"

"Just inject it please. The entire cartridge." Roy's discomfort was making it difficult for him to even get those few words out.

She pulled up the sleeve of his polo t-shirt and did just that.

"Will compressing the abdomen help?"

Not waiting for a response, she gently started pressing his abdomen. He wasn't sure if it was helping, but he was glad to have her there.

Half an hour later, Roy was better.

"That was scary."

"Been there often," he replied. But Anya could tell his nonchalance was forced.

"Are you allergic to seafood? Is it sprue? Gluten intolerance?"

Roy smiled despite his pain. This was so typical of Anya—wanting quick answers to everything.

"Give me a few moments, Anya."

Once he felt a little better, he continued, "Gluten is just one of the many things that I am allergic to. Ever since I was an infant, I have had allergies to different foods. When I was a baby, infant formula food would set off a severe pain. As I grew, the list of foods that were triggers became longer and more mysterious. The textbooks describe specific allergies, but in my case, none of those seemed to fit. The doctors agreed I had a very sensitive gut mucosa. The allergies were most severe in early childhood and the allergic reactions were very strong—even needing hospitalisation. Each meal was a challenge. No one knew what would agree with me and what wouldn't. Gradually, we figured out what food was safe for me, and I began to stick to those. Now, I usually know what to avoid—which is most things that normal people love to eat. But sometimes, it takes me by surprise. Like this time."

Anya listened intently. So that explained Roy's fussiness and quirkiness with food. Why he hunted for fruits and juices and ice lollies. And why he quietly reached for his own granola bars before they checked out new restaurants.

Roy sensed that Anya was thinking about him. And he didn't want her to pity him. He hated when anyone did that.

"You almost carted me off to the Cath lab." He jibed.

"Of course. I needed to rule out a coronary."

"But you forgot one thing. Take a good history. Listen to the patient. Especially if the patient is a doctor himself."

Anya laughed. It was a relief to see Roy get better. "So, is the patient advising himself some rest?"

"Hmm, yes. But I need to check some documents that Naik has sent across. I must close the oxygen pipeline supply orders ASAP."

"I am sure it can wait." Anya shook her head.

"I will just take a peek at the papers, then, I will head home."

"Do you want me to hang around?"

"Thanks, but I am good."

"Maybe I should get a nursing officer to check in on you in a while?"

"How about I promise to call you in case I don't feel better?"

She was reluctant to leave, but she knew that arguing with Roy was pointless.

Roy took small sips of water and watched her leave.

Roy had put up a brave front with her, but the severity of this attack had unnerved him. Even though the epinephrine had acted instantly, and he had stopped quivering in pain, a dull ache would remain for a while. Likewise, the painful memories that were the legacy of the rare and complex illness that had clouded his growing up years, eclipsed his happiness and finally resulted in a painful breakup.

He could feel himself sinking in the abyss of darkness that the memories had opened. Fear, anger, pain, guilt, frustration—the concoction of feelings that he had buried for years would be waiting him at the deep bottom of this abyss.

He tried to overcome the memory of himself as a little child in the stark, antiseptic hospital room. He remembered wearing the hospital gown that was too loose for his sickly physique. The hushed whispers from outside, the fatigue in his father's eyes, his mother's face lined with anxiety—everything had been terrifying. The soft mattress had felt hard. He had shivered despite the blanket on his legs. Was this what it felt like to be dying? He had wondered.

Even after decades, these flashbacks were a part of his life. He began skip counting—a coping mechanism from childhood, which he had forgotten about till he spoke about it in a recent counselling session.

"Why did you stop counting if it brought you relief?" the therapist had asked him.

"That's for kids. I am old enough to deal with stuff without it."

"Maybe you can try counting for the little boy in that image?"

It had made a difference. And he had stuck with the sessions which he had reluctantly started.

He waited for the pain to settle and thought back to more snippets of the sessions.

"I am lucky to have survived my illness. And fortunate to have had such a supportive, loving family. There are many who are not as fortunate. I should not feel sorry for myself."

"There is no rule book for feelings, Roy, which tells us what to feel. For each of us, our feelings are valid. We needn't compare them to anyone or anything. Instead of questioning your feelings, try to sit with them. Try not to push them away; and allow yourself to feel them. You may find that it is possible to hold space for even the contradictory feelings of gratitude and sorrow simultaneously."

"But there are so many people whose troubles are more than mine."

"Doctors quantify everything, don't they? There is even a scale for physical pain. But such a hierarchy does not exist for emotional pain. Grief, which is felt differently by each one of us, is not a contest. We don't need to decide if one person's grief is more or less than another's. You lost so much because of your illness—your childhood, your friendships, dreams, even love. The good things in your life are a blessing, no doubt. But they don't have to be a foil to your loss. Loss is loss. Pain is pain. Feeling it, mourning it is as important as being grateful for the good stuff. Distracting ourselves from our pain does make things bearable for a while, and that's okay too. But, in the long term, denial doesn't do us good. If we stop ourselves from feeling our pain, it festers within. It will make us bitter and brittle and will eventually break us. Don't stop yourself from feeling the pain."

The next couple of weeks had been hard...damn hard. Sitting with his feelings had been very difficult. It was as if his feelings were shards of glass—some with raw jagged edges, and others which were sharp and pointed. All the different types of pains listed in medical textbooks—acute, dull, radiating, stabbing, burning—seemed to be happening all at once. But that had changed, gradually. Now they didn't hurt as much. Perhaps they had been blunted by familiarity or acceptance or a mixture of both.

He looked at the jar of seashells on his desk. That was another throwback to childhood—or missed childhood, as he realised now. His parents, struggling to raise a child with a chronic illness, had not had time to indulge in vacations. There were so many things that he had missed out on. Small things which became big because he had never done them. While he didn't resent having missed out on things like picking seashells, impromptu excursions with friends or making a dive for the chocolate decoration on birthday cakes, he had always been aware that his childhood was different from theirs. Speaking about these in therapy had helped. It was in college that he had first visited the seaside in Mumbai. It was an unforgettable experience. There were so many feelings and thoughts that came to his mind when he saw the sea—but what always stood out was their mixed nature. The distant fury of the ocean could turn into gentleness at the seashore. The vastness of the ocean was a reminder of how small he was. It was humbling in a strangely relieving way—if he was small, so must his troubles be. At the beach, he felt a calmness descend upon him; at the same time, it was an exciting place to be. He would wait for low tide and then quietly slip seashells into his pockets. Then he would rush in to experience the waves of the high tide behind him. He had felt like a child. He still did when he was at the beach.

"Who decides if something is childish? And does it matter, Roy? If picking up and collecting seashells is making you happy, what's wrong with it?" the therapist had asked him.

And so, here in Goa, he continued collecting seashells. Like the little boy that he had been. The one that still lurked inside behind this adult version of his.

He reached for the files next to him and began making notations in the margins.

The abyss seemed to give up on him in a while. The pain subsided too. That was how it always was. The pain was like the sea that he loved so much. It came and went in waves which were hard to predict. You couldn't foretell its ferocity. It could seem easy to navigate on some days and could overwhelm you on others. However far on land you were, it was a reality that you would be face to face with it someday. Even when you couldn't see it, you were always aware of its presence, and how it could sweep you away.

He thought about his new friends—Anya and Neel both were struggling with pain that they never put into words. Yet, like a force field around them, their pain made its presence felt. He hoped Neel would finally find the courage to listen to his own self, the inner voice that he had ignored for so long that it might feel like that of a stranger.

Despite Anya's constant efforts to run from her pain, it was imprinted on her face. It was what stopped her eyes from lighting up even when she laughed. The shock of losing her sister had been more than Anya could ever reconcile to. But she needed to allow herself to feel her grief. To allow herself to fall in the abyss, however scary the thought may be.

13

Latin Quarters

The sunny October morning was perfect for the trio to visit the Latin Quarters which was known for its Portuguese style bungalows with bright coloured walls and intricate designs on curved railings. The old-world charm of the place made Anya feel that she had stepped back in time. She realised that this was what visitors to their home in Old Delhi—or Dilli-6 as the area was colloquially called—meant when they commented on the nostalgic vibe. These large verandas would be the place for long evening conversations. Conversations like the ones her grandmother would have with the neighbours in sunny winters on the rooftops of the houses in Chandni Chowk that hung over narrow streets. And the ones she and Zoya would have while taking in the warmth of the winter sun.

Roy was sharing the vignettes that he had picked up from the travel guide with Anya. "The houses are painted each year after the monsoons."

They stopped at the 18th June Road and Anya called out to Neel.

"Wait, Neel, Mr. Encyclopaedia here hasn't told us about this interesting street name yet."

"On this date, Ram Manohar Lohia called for the liberation of..."

Roy stopped on seeing Anya's twinkling eyes. She was ready to burst out in laughter.

Neel walked on, leaving them to continue their usual repartee.

"Why waste money on a heritage walk, when we have Roy giving us free nuggets of information!"

"Just for that, I won't tell you the name of the most famous eatery around here!"

"Hey, that's not fair. I am hungry already."

"Nothing new about that! Can we look around a little before you start looking for places to eat?"

The haphazardly winding streets branched out into maze-like thinner cobblestone streets, and they ambled along before coming across a quaint bakery.

"This is the oldest and most famous bakery I promised to tell you about. They are known best for their delicious Bebinca," Roy said as Anya looked longingly through the windows.

"Go on, I know you can't wait to try it." Roy nudged her.

Anya laughed and stepped inside to place her order. The multi-layered dessert was as delicious as it looked and smelt.

"Hey, there is the art gallery you mentioned, Roy. Should we check it out?" Neel called out.

"Art gallery?" Anya was surprised, but before she could say anything Roy had nodded a yes.

The art gallery had an alluring deep blue exterior with white window frames. The soft grey walls inside were a perfect backdrop for showcasing artworks. Neel had found the perfect place for experimenting with his photography. Roy began looking at the paintings that lined the wall, discussing them with the curator, and taking note of some of the names in his phone.

"Football, trauma surgery, art appreciation—that is an unusual combination." Anya remarked.

Roy smiled. That broad smile which reached the corner of his eyes—not the sarcastic one that he curled up his lips for.

"Yeah. Actually, it's for mom. She would love this place."

"She is into art?"

"She used to paint a lot. She has won many awards too."

Even in these few words, Anya could feel the huge affection that he had for his mother. So far, he had spoken mostly of his father; and their shared passion for football. The energy with which he spoke of those was replaced by a palpable tenderness at the mention of his mother.

"That's lovely. What medium does she use?"

"She stopped."

There was a sharpness in those words—an abrupt change from their light-hearted banter. And then, silence. This was Roy's trademark silence, a brooding heaviness that would creep up on him at the most unexpected times. Like now.

Then, as if he suddenly remembered that he wasn't alone, he added, "Got busy with other things in life."

Anya simply said, "She could start now. Again."

Roy flinched. This was why he didn't share too much of himself with anyone. Everyone had a solution; a quickly available, easy solution. If life was so simple, there wouldn't be any questions or problems, would there? Yet, there was something in Anya's softened tone that made him listen to her.

"Roy, my mother always nurtured a dream of having her own fashion studio. But the responsibilities that life brings didn't give her a chance to realise her ambition. Now, after decades, she is finally doing that. Why don't you get your mom to take up the paint brush again?"

Though Anya had told Roy about Sumita's fashion studio, she was keeping the rest to herself. It had been Zoya's idea that Sumita launch her own design studio in Gurgaon. *"Gurgaon's clientele would be ideal for mom's awesome fusion wear."* Zoya had always been their mother's champion and cheerleader. Now, the studio would bear her sister's name.

"You think it's that simple?"

The words rose in Roy's mind, but the tear at the corner of Anya's eye stopped him from saying them out loud. He let it go.

They walked along, taking in the art works in silence. Anya tried not to think about Zoya—or her parents—or the fact that her family would soon be leaving the house she had grown up in. Roy was lost in thought about dreams that never came true—his, and his mother's. Usually, these thoughts would linger in both their minds. But today they didn't take up as much space as they usually did. Being in each other's company helped them quell those demons, at least for a while.

"It says 'bookstore' on the right. I will check it out." Anya said.

"Sure. I will browse through the art works upstairs."

The corridor opened into a large hall done up in natural shades of brown. The aroma of roasted coffee beans mingled with the distinctive smell of old, thumbed through paperbacks—an ambience as perfect as the tagline for the café—'Fresh coffee. Pre-loved books'.

The sight of so many old books was a throwback to the numerous Sunday mornings that Anya—and Zoya—had spent at the Darya Ganj flea market. The pleasure of finding a book that you loved was unmatchable. Zoya would say that with used books, you felt connected to the previous readers, like kindred spirits. Her sister, ever the romantic at heart, loved to check if any of them had a name or a note written in them. Or an inscription or a date. Zoya loved weaving stories based on those inscriptions. Maybe the books had been gifted by a suitor; or a lover's tiff had made the owner give up the book? Or maybe the books would unite soulmates searching for their favourite books, just like the movie *Serendipity*? For Anya, not prone to her sister's sentimentality, it was an opportunity to bargain down to the last rupee. If the flea market had sections like a bookstore, the sisters would have disappeared in different corners and met only at the billing counter, a few hours later. But the eclectic mix of titles on display meant than they would search for the titles together—calling out to each other when they found a title that would interest the other. Anya had no patience for mushy romance books that Zoya loved, the kind in which a happily ever after ending was a given. Give her a gory thriller any day.

The two sisters had held very different views on love and relationships through their teenage and college years. Breakups and new interests were common for Anya, who would regularly attend parties where she could find the right dates. Zoya preferred her books and solitude and maintained that love would happen when it had to.

"Zoydi, don't you want to find that someone special? If you don't get out and meet people, how will that happen?"

"Anni… You mean soulmates? Of course, who doesn't want to find their soulmate? I am sure that if we are destined to meet our true love, we will."

"Zoydi, sitting in this run-down medical college campus canteen, bleary eyed with fatigue, there is no way you will find them. We can't leave it to destiny."

Zoya had sighed. "You can't go out and find love. It's not something that can be hunted for. Love finds you. When it must."

"Yeah, like at the top of the Empire State building." Anya had retorted sarcastically, referring to Zoya's favourite movie *Sleepless in Seattle*. Zoya was a hopeless romantic—though whenever the topic came up, she preferred to call herself a hopeful romantic.

"Yes, exactly," Zoya said, softly. Anya sighed. Her sister was one of the prettiest girls on the campus, and there would be many suitors for her. But Zoya would always shy away from their advances. Anya didn't know what Zoya was looking for, what imaginary patterns she kept drawing between stars and what mysterious sign she was waiting for.

"Zoydi, I am not going to hang about waiting till old age for this magical event to occur."

"Then what are you going to do?"

"I will attend all the college festivals. I will have fun, dance and find dates there. Can I borrow your pleated skirt?" Zoya had laughed. And like always, Zoya had let Anya raid her wardrobe.

Just thinking about how those Sunday mornings would never be a part of her life again brought a tear to Anya's eyes.

Upstairs, Roy continued to think about his mother. Truth be told, breaking up with Denise had opened his eyes about his mother's dream for painting. Radha's paintings had always decorated their home, but he had recently realised that his mother had nursed—and then given up on—her ambitious dream of becoming a professional artist after pursuing a traditional career for a few years. If she had continued with her painting journey, she would have been as accomplished as the artists who were featured in the gallery. He paused at a small kiosk which stocked art supplies. And he recalled Anya's words: "She can start again." Maybe she could, after all. He bought some paints and brushes and quickly put them away in his backpack. His mother's birthday was round the corner.

Anya found Neel in the café reading an *Asterix* comic and sipping his coffee. Anya picked up hers from the counter and stirred the sugar carefully, from the side, taking care not to disturb the top frothy layer. Zoya hated disrupting the design on that. Especially if it was a heart.

Roy also joined them with his espresso.

They continued their walk along the tiny streets until they came to a step well with a large rooster on top. The rays of the setting sun were bouncing off the rooster giving it a diffuse glow. The red bricks of the stepwell had a chalky white outline and it looked as if it were out of a fairy tale.

"So, if this was a real wishing well, what would you wish for?" Neel asked.

"Neel, a well cannot make wishes come true."

Roy's tone had an unexpected edge to it. Anya couldn't help but agree with Roy—what good were wishes when life dealt you such unfair blows?

"I would rather imagine the amount of money at the bottom of the well. That would make several wishes come true, wouldn't it?' This was Roy's typical style—humour with a tinge of darkness and truth. Roy continued his tirade. "Actually, we should have a well where we can dump our wishes and our dreams. Because that is where they will end up anyway."

Anya was surprised. Roy could be aloof and sarcastic, but he wasn't usually this cynical. He was choking on the emotions that he hadn't allowed to surface when he spoke about his mother in the art gallery. She knew how sensitive he really was. And how he tried to hide it.

Neel figured that Roy's bitterness was not directed towards him, but at life. He looked across at his friend.

"But Roy, the knowledge that dreams don't always come true; that life will always have other plans for us doesn't stop us from making wishes, does it? After all, wishes and dreams mean that we still have the capacity to hope, don't they? And what would life be without hope?"

Roy was silent as he composed himself.

"Anyway, we can plan an expedition to fish for the hidden treasure at the bottom of the well sometime." Neel had had enough of the serious moments.

Anya smiled.

"Yeah, buddy." Roy slapped him on the back and laughed. "Now, that's a plan to look forward to."

"So, what do we check out next?"

"The shops with the Azulejo tiles."

Anya selected a few tiles for her mother to display in her new studio. "We will ship them to your address, ma'am." The cashier handed her a paper and a pencil.

She paused for a moment. In a few months, the house in Chandni Chowk wouldn't be home anymore. She would be writing a different address—it seemed impossible, but it was true. She shrugged the thought away and wrote down the address.

They walked back—each at their own pace, and in their own thoughts; comfortable with each other's presence and company; not feeling the need for small talk to fill the space between them.

A golden glow now softly descended on them as the three returned to the H-of-H campus, after a day well spent. A day where the past had been with them, but had shared space with the present in an unexpected tranquillity.

14

Pizza and Pain

"Dinner? We can order in from the new pizza place." Neel asked when they pulled up at the residences block. "My place?"

"Sounds good," Anya replied, but she didn't miss Roy's hesitation. She figured he wanted to go back to his refrigerator.

Anya was confused about food when she was with Roy. It was a challenge to find eateries that offered fruits and veggies. While he didn't seem to mind her checking out other menus, it didn't seem right to gorge on food while he just looked on. She knew coffee shops worked for him. And bakeries were the most difficult. Juice bars and ice lollies were safe zones too, she had learnt. It was strange how food, which was a comfort and a stress buster for her, was a restriction and a terrible inconvenience for him.

"We could go to your place instead, if you are more comfortable with that?"

"Okay." Roy replied.

Roy's apartment was simple and uncluttered. The kitchen was stocked with a Juice Ninja and many fridgeware containers.

"Anya, which pizza would you like?" Neel called out.

Roy was warming up his meal in the microwave.

"Hmm, one with as many toppings as possible."

Roy smiled.

"Cold coffee anyone?" Roy called out.

"Yes." Anya replied.

"Not for me. I will have a soda." Neel called out.

Anya heard Roy run the blender with ice cubes to crush the ice. The sound of the ice cubes being crushed reminded her of her and Zoya's unsuccessful attempts at making ice lollies at home. They would not be able to hold the ice on a stick and would end up making a sherbet out of the melting ice and flavoured syrup. She shut her eyes and waited for the moment to pass.

Neel and Anya devoured the pizza as soon as it arrived and made to leave.

"Do you need help with clearing up?"

"No, I got it. You both carry on."

Roy cleared the pizza boxes. It had been nice of Anya to suggest that they go over to his apartment. He wondered if she found it difficult having to find a place with a menu that worked for him when they hung out. Anya enjoyed food. He was sure there were a few places she might have checked out if he hadn't been around. Everything in his life, since the time he was a child, had centred around his allergies. Frequent absence from school and being singled out meant that he had grown up to be a loner. Roy had learnt to stick to foods that were safe for him; the granola bars his father customised for him were a huge help. In spite of the popularity that came with being a football champion, he remained an introvert. He had learnt that explaining his allergies didn't help. Most people didn't understand how serious the matter was. Those who did usually pitied him.

That was why Roy didn't have too many close friends and been in just a handful of casual relationships. Relationships where he had never been comfortable to open up about all the things that made him who he was. And when he had finally done that with Denise, it had all gone wrong.

The bitter memories of the breakup were intruding on the happiness that a day spent with friends had brought.

What had started as a relationship based on mutual interests like following Formula1 racing and Climate Change activism had become a series of arguments about how everything in the relationship was according to his needs; never hers. How they could never do any fun stuff because of Roy's food constraints.

"You are so boring and high maintenance."

"Maybe it's best to take a break from each other, Roy. I need space to be myself."

"It is always about you."

The words had left a raw wound. Often, he found himself wondering if this were true. If he really was self-absorbed and selfish. His health issues had occupied his childhood and his parents' lives too. His father had given up his career and his mother her painting. Then again, when he was in senior school, the long hospitalisation had taken up everyone's time and energy.

He sighed. Why was the melancholy setting in after such a nice day?

The notifications pinged. Neel was sharing photos from today and Roy found himself looking at the ones with Anya in them longer than the rest of them. She had got on his nerves when they had first met. It was later that he had realised that she wasn't stuck up or difficult. Her anger was both a symptom of the pain she felt, and an escape too.

15

Travel Plans

It was just 11 am but Roy already had a long list of tasks to attend to. He decided to take a mid-morning coffee break and went to the café. Anya was there too.

"Hey! Long shift?"

"Hi! Just managed to get away from the ER. How have you been?"

"Good. And busy."

"Filling in for the surgical team on Sundays?"

Roy nodded. After Tess's surgery, he had begun working on his confidence. Anya had persuaded him to cover the OR on Sundays.

"Anya, we need you to interview paramedics for the emergency room for the upcoming hospital locations. The interviews are scheduled for next week at Delhi.

"Hey, I can't take time off."

"Yes, you can, Anya. This is important too."

Anya didn't think that travelling to Delhi was a great idea; especially now. With Diwali round the corner, her parents would insist on her spending the festival at home.

"Roy, maybe we can shortlist the candidates, and do the interviews later?"

Before Roy could reply, Neel walked over to their table with his usual diet soda can.

"What's up?"

"Roy is packing me off for interviews to Delhi." Anya cribbed.

"Maybe Neel and you could travel together, Anya. He is also taking time off," Roy said, quietly.

"Hey, you never mentioned that!" Anya turned to Neel. "What has been keeping you so busy these days?"

Anya had sensed that there was something going on with her goofy, entertaining friend. She didn't call him Neel the dreamer, for nothing. Though he had tried to pass it off as being busy with work, there had been a subtle change in him. She was curious about what it was that was keeping her friend pre-occupied—it had a good vibe to it.

"Just a short trip." Neel changed the topic.

"Roy, why don't you take a vacation? We could hang out together."

It had turned out to be a coincidence that Roy's home was also in Gurgaon, the suburb of Delhi, where Neel's parents lived. And where Anya's family would be moving to soon.

"Too much happening here, Neel. We must get the maternity wing started by the middle of November."

Here too, Anya sensed something unspoken but deeply felt. Unlike Neel's secrecy though, this felt darker; almost restive. Despite knowing about Roy's food allergies, and his passion for surgery, sometimes she felt like she didn't know him at all.

16

Delhi Ahoy

Neel and Anya were on their way to the airport. Neel's chatter as he pointed out cloud formations was a welcome distraction for Anya. Distrait and preoccupied with her thoughts, she didn't pick up the tinge of nervousness in her friend's conversation.

As she walked towards the check-in counters, Anya steeled herself. There were too many memories waiting to greet her in Delhi; especially those from another Diwali. Just two years ago, the family had been together to celebrate the festival. It had been a lovely, magical time—full of surprises, dreams and promises. A time that would never return. As if that wasn't enough, this trip was a stark reminder of the fact that her family would soon be moving out of the house where she and Zoya had grown up. Every time her father shared updates about the new home in Gurgaon, she would tune herself out of the conversation. Now, there would be no escape.

"I pre-booked a window seat." Neel grinned.

"Yeah, I guessed as much."

"Roy been snitching?"

"Just giving me a heads up about having you as a fellow traveller."

Roy, who had travelled with Neel for work recently, had warned her that Neel would be busy watching the clouds. As the aircraft would soar above, cutting through the clouds, Neel would be lost in his thoughts and would make no conversation at all. Anya had laughed.

They took their seats.

"So, what are your plans for this trip?"

Anya was surprised when Neel didn't reply immediately.

"Haven't really planned much."

"Neel, just hanging around at home doesn't seem like you."

But Neel was already immersed in his dreamy world of clouds.

Not for the first time, Neel reminded Anya of Zoya. Like her sister, he was generous, lovable—and lost deep in his inner world. It felt as if he was always searching, rather yearning, for something. She didn't know what that something was. Often, he himself didn't seem to know either. He had been even more abstracted than usual the last couple of weeks.

Anya saw her father waiting as soon as they exited the airport.

"Papa. I told you not to bother with coming to the airport."

"Since when do I have to listen to you, my lovely daughter?" He hugged her.

She introduced Neel.

"Can I give you a ride?"

"No, thanks uncle."

It was not just the traffic that was making the ride home seem formidable.

She listened to her father tell her how the markets were crowded with the festival rush; that this year the rains had continued into October, the usual waterlogging, and how the share market was performing. It was as if he thought that chatting incessantly would keep the memories of the airport ride from two years ago at bay. Anya began scrolling on her phone and tried to think about something else. Anything other than Zoya's last trip home, on Diwali the year before last.

Her father was now talking about the new home in Gurgaon. He really seemed to think that if he filled all the space and minutes of the journey with words, Zoya's absence would not find place to make itself felt. As if that was possible. A void as big as the universe now occupied her heart—and soul—and nothing could ever fill it.

Their WhatsApp group pinged. Neel had shared a picture of the arrival lounge which he had clicked while they were waiting near the baggage belts. It was a fantastic shot, which showed people as fuzzy silhouettes and the large hoardings behind in focus. 'Delhi rocks', Neel had captioned the picture.

"Missing Delhi, especially the kebabs from Karim's (lip-smacking emoji)." Roy had replied.

"Ha! Ha! Given how you don't eat them, all you must be missing would be the smell of the meat mingling with the ghee." Neel had quickly replied.

"True. Missing the vibe of the place."

The chat helped to distract her on the long drive.

Neel continued sharing pictures.

'Home', the caption to the next one read. It was a row house, with a brick wall façade.

Neel quickly followed up his message with the 'highly annoyed' emoji. Anya didn't know why Neel had this odd bitterness and simmering resentment towards his family.

"Beeji insisted on waiting up for you."

Whatever the circumstances, mention of her dear grandmother always brought a smile to Anya's face. The video calls that she made to Beeji hadn't been compensation enough for the sweetly comforting smell of Nivea that always accompanied the elderly woman.

It was midnight when they finally reached Chandni Chowk. Fairy lights in a crisscross pattern covered the lane which led to their house. Anya felt a stab of anger. Last Diwali, in solidarity with their loss, there had been no community celebrations in the neighbourhood. But did the end of the traditional mourning period of one year mean that everything could go back to the way it always had? Grief didn't come with an expiry date, after which you could toss it in the trash can like a mouldy loaf of leftover bread. With so much darkness in their hearts, what would her parents be feeling seeing these lights of festivity?

But before she could persist with her indignation, she was enveloped in hugs from her mother and grandmother.

"You are looking so tired."

"She has become so thin, *pakka* not eating properly. No desi ghee in the food there."

Ghar ka khana and desi ghee were embedded in her grandmother's psyche, and Anya prepared herself for gaining a couple of kilograms in the coming week. She would need to join Roy in the gym once she went back to Goa. For now, though, at 1 am, the four of them sat in the courtyard, sipping ginger tea and enjoying home-made gulab jamuns.

In the morning, Anya woke up to the smell of parathas. The crisp parathas filled with mashed potatoes spiced with coriander, ginger and raw mango powder were awesome. The melting butter and the cold yoghurt that accompanied them mingled in her mouth. When she was growing up, it had seemed magical the way Beeji could take any vegetable, even leftover ones, and turn it into the most amazing meal by making a parathas out of it and serving it with a dollop of white butter.

Beeji watched Anya eat, and quietly asked, "Do you remember how surprised Zoya's friend was when she saw me add sugar to crumbled roti? Sugar-bread she called it! She gobbled it up!"

All of Anya's resolve not to let the memories surface was broken with that single reminiscence of Laura eating *roti ki choori*.

MEMORIES FROM ANOTHER LIFETIME...

Two years ago, Zoya had come home for Diwali. She had called to tell them that she was bringing a friend with her, Laura. Laura, a journalist, would spend a few days with them before travelling to Kerala for research on her book on medical tourism.

The house was buzzing with activity. For Anya, the excitement was doubled because of the secret Zoya had shared with her a few days back on the phone. Zoya, her reticent, reserved sister had finally fallen in love. But Zoya had stopped short of telling her dear sister more. Not only that, Zoya had asked Anya to keep this development from the rest of the family for now. Zoya, the perpetual romantic at heart, wanted to share her love story with Anya in person, not on a long-distance call. The suspense had been driving Anya crazy, and she couldn't wait to have her sister to herself and hear all the details.

When they reached home in the early hours of the morning, Zoya, Laura and Anya chatted into the night making plans for the Diwali celebrations before finally falling asleep. A few hours later, Anya's sleep was disturbed by the lights on in the room opposite to theirs—the one they had spruced up for Laura. Jet lag, Anya had assumed and gone back to sleep. Zoya's upper berth of their bunk bed was empty too, but Anya didn't know that.

The preparations for the festival were in full swing.

"Mom, can I wear a saree from your collection on Diwali?" Zoya asked Sumita.

"I will also wear one. And I will pick first," Anya interjected quickly.

Before Sumita could reply, Zoya—always looking out for Anya—spoke, "Of course, Anni. You pick first."

Sumita smiled at her daughters.

"Laura would also like to try wearing one." Zoya continued.

"Of course. Let her select one she likes, and I will get the tailor to adjust one of my blouses."

Laura was very keen to celebrate the traditional Indian festival with them.

It was finally Diwali evening. They would all be getting together in the courtyard soon for the rituals.

"Zoydi, Zoydi...which of these earrings looks better?" Anya wanted her sister's involvement and approval in even the smallest of things.

Anya found Zoya in Laura's room, rummaging through a box of costume jewellery, searching for the right accessories for the saree that Laura had draped. Laura's fair freckled skin contrasted perfectly with the deep indigo of the silk saree. Her light brown hair fell on the green blouse around her shoulders. She looked beautiful. But what held Anya's attention was Zoya. Zoya was looking at Laura, her face transfixed in rapture. Anya had never seen her sister like that. The emotions on her face were unmistakable. Zoya was in love. With Laura. How could Anya have missed this?

"Anni, what's up?" Zoya had just noticed that Anya was in the room with them.

Now it was Zoya's turn to take in Anya's expressions. She knew that Anya knew. It was a relief. Keeping a secret from her sister was not something she wanted to do, but she had not been sure how to share this important part of herself. Zoya had spent a decade fighting her confusions and her eventual realisation about her sexuality. Her journey of questioning and understanding had entailed embracing herself and trying to escape herself in equal measure. It had also influenced all her decisions so far. Zoya had a deep desire to experience motherhood and have a family of her own. The care and affection that she had showered on Anya had been the beginning—or the manifestation of a very strong maternal instinct. One that Zoya hoped to realise one day by having her own family. But, given her homosexuality, it was a dream that she wouldn't be able to realise in India. So, she had decided to move to the US and forge a new life for herself. In New York, she had settled into her new apartment and job, but something had still seemed missing. Until that moment, on what would otherwise have been a usual day. Zoya had stopped for a coffee takeaway on her way to work. Walking out with her tall Styrofoam glass in one hand, she had crossed Laura, who was just entering the cafe. For Zoya, a firm believer in fate and the power of the universe, that single moment was enough. She had fallen in love. That moment was magical as the slow dance scene in *The Notebook*. The doors had shut behind her, but even the chilly February winds of New York on her face could not take away the warmth that she had felt. She was unperturbed that she knew nothing about the tall, blonde woman in a long trench coat whose path she had just crossed. She had driven on to work to deliver those tiny little babies who filled her heart with joy. Later, in the day, during a meeting, the hospital director had introduced them to a medical journalist who wanted to write about their hospital as part of her series on maternal health care. Laura Arlington. If this wasn't serendipity at work, what was? Zoya and Laura had made eye contact, held each other's gaze and recognised each other as missing parts of their own selves. The next few months had been the most intense, yet most calming ones in Zoya's life. Zoya, who was always lost in the world of stars, had found her pole star. For Laura, who was struggling with being ostracised by her family, it felt like a homecoming. This trip to Delhi, together, was a huge step in their relationship. Just one step short of announcing their plans for the next year—marriage.

Anya's eyes gleamed with happiness for her sister as she hugged Laura and Zoya. Zoya had a good feeling about this. In her younger sister, she had a comrade she could trust and a friend she could count on.

The next few days were filled with happiness. They had planned the immediate future and looked forward to the distant one.

17

Darkness and Light

The interviews had been concluded and now, on the day before Diwali, Anya found time hanging heavy on her hands. This was the busiest time of the year for her family's dry fruit business. To distract herself, she took over the mundane tasks that the festival brings. Anya ran her hands over the packaging of the corporate hampers. The handcrafted wrapping with a collage of brocade fabrics sewn together had been designed by Sumita, who had been nudged into it by Zoya. It was strange how meaningless things like gift boxes could conjure heart-rending memories. Memories of Zoya and Anya labelling the packets and of Anya getting frustrated when she couldn't copy Zoya's neat, evenly spaced-out cursive writing. And Zoya lovingly admonishing her with her loving wisdom, *"Anni... Don't try to copy me, or anyone. Just be yourself."* Words which bore the weight of a heavy rock, put across with the gentleness of a feather. That was how Zoya always had been.

Struggling to control her emotions, Anya reminded herself of the years when Zoya would be busy in her studies and wouldn't be around for festivals. That was the thing—all you needed to do was pretend that Zoya was away, she told herself. Otherwise, the pain was too much to bear. Especially here, back home, where she was face to face with the suffering of her parents and grandmother. So many times, Anya had heard Beeji bitterly ask the gods she prayed to everyday. "Why did you not take me instead?" and had heard her mother sob uncontrollably in Beeji's arms.

Anya finished checking the labels on the packages and glanced at Beeji who was sitting across the courtyard, in her room, with the doors open—as they always were. How would Beeji be feeling at having to leave the house she had grown up—and grown old in? Even the thought was too much to handle for Anya. Right now, even the ER with all its stress, chaos, heartbreak, tribulations, pain, and grief, seemed to be a better option than being here, at home.

From her room across the courtyard, Beeji called out to Anya.

"Come, let me give you a head massage."

Beeji took a few drops of the home-made oil onto her palms and tenderly began massaging Anya's hair. Her curly, frizzy hair was always a challenge, unlike Zoya's soft brown hair. Sighing softly, Beeji worked the oil into Anya's scalp. Her dear grandchild, who had been so full of life, now held the entire world's grief and anger within her slender frame, she thought. It would help her to talk, vent and cry it out. But despite all her apparent exuberance, this was how Anya had always been. In difficult times, she could be quiet and reserved; and when deeply troubled, impenetrable. In those times, she would respond only to Zoya. And there was no Zoya now.

Head massage done, Beeji wiped her hands and began gentling caressing Anya's temples and forehead. She spoke softly, hoping her words would be a soothing balm to Anya's pain.

"Anya, life must be lived. Till the day that we are breathing and present on this earth, we must live. We do not have any choice in that. The Almighty decides the moment when we stop living, and we cannot challenge that."

She felt Anya catch her breath and continued.

"I know you cannot imagine celebration in a world without Zoya. But we must all come together and do whatever needs to be done on this day."

"Beeji, when no one's heart is in this, why do it?"

"My child, sometimes the heart needs an anchor, something to tie its meandering thoughts down. See your father, the only time he has smiled is since you have come."

"And Ma, Beeji? When did Ma smile?"

Beeji was silent. Anya was right. Sumita had retreated into silence since Zoya's death. The scant succour that Sumita found was in Beeji. Sumita would allow Beeji to hug her, hold her close, even gently disentangle her hair and oil it for her. She could have been a little girl again, searching for the comforting touch of a mother—one that had not been in her fate. Beeji, who had lived through loss of people and things in her life, seemed to transmit her resilience, and tenderness, to Sumita—a little every day; just enough for Sumita to survive until the next day.

Beeji took Anya's face in her wrinkled hands, ignoring the tears falling furiously. There was nothing she wouldn't do for her family's pain to end. There was nothing she could do for her family's pain to end.

The next morning, the morning of the festival of lights, Anya pretended to sleep in. Even the wafting scent of parathas couldn't give her the courage to go outside and face her family on one of the most important days of the year. It was almost lunch time when Subodh knocked on her room.

"Anya, will you help your mother with the preparations? She must get the things together for the puja at the new house."

Subodh was sitting by her side on the bed, straightening the pillows as he always did, when he would come to tuck the girls in for the night.

His tone, pleading and helpless, made Anya go red in the face. Of course, all of this would be toughest on Sumita.

"Yes, Papa, of course."

Last year, the house had been devoid of decorations. But this was the last time that the house would witness any festival, and Subodh had decided that tradition would be followed this year. Whenever they looked back, he hoped they remembered it looking beautiful and welcoming; and not dark and filled with sadness. Beeji had agreed. "After all, memories are all that remains when all is done and gone. And it is those memories that we will look towards whenever we need strength," she had advised gently.

This year, as tradition mandated, they would also be doing the Diwali rituals at the new house in Gurgaon. Anya pushed the lump in her throat deeper as she watched the preparations. She just wanted the evening and her trip back home to end soon.

Sumita was in the kitchen staring vacantly as Beeji was overseeing the arrangements. Anya hugged her mother even as she seethed inside. When the gods above had meted out so much unkindness to their family, why seek their blessings? Did God even exist? What kind of God would take away Zoya from this world? Wasn't it the job of the Almighty to do good by everyone?

Just a few more hours, she consoled herself, and then this charade would end.

She couldn't wait to get back to H-of-H, to Goa, and to the carefree banter of her friendship with Neel and Roy. As if on cue, the group notification buzzed.

It was Neel. "We could catch up if you are anywhere near Gurgaon sometime today."

Neel's home was not far from the new house.

"Cool! We are going to the new house today evening itself." She texted back. This seemed like the perfect way to get away from the depressive evening that this was going to be.

The afternoon slumber led to evening. The house gradually came alive. It was a gentle, reluctant stirring; tentative at first, bearing the shadow of Zoya's passing. As the lights came on, the oil lamps began to flicker and the moonless night shined bright, Anya reconciled to not being able to escape anymore. Beeji had changed into a new salwar kameez. Even Sumita was wearing lipstick—a light shade but one that, nonetheless, took the attention away from her tired and sunken eyes. Anya hadn't packed anything festive and pulled out a short white silk blouse from Sumita's wardrobe. It looked perfect with her peach palazzos. She did have her mother's sense of style after all.

The open-to-the-sky courtyard was not just the physical centre of the house, but also the nucleus of their lives—so many mundane as well as special events had unfolded here. It was a repository of many memories, emotions and moments. The large pillars which supported the high ceiling had given strength to the family, and the delicate old-fashioned carvings on them grace and dignity. The bright paint of the doors of the rooms which opened into it had brought them cheer, and the tulsi plant in the courtyard was a reminder of the power of belief. The villa they were moving into was large and modern, but could it make up for all these? Anya wondered, as she thought of the wonderful times spent here with friends and family. Times when simple things like playing hide and seek, chatting with cousins, taking in the smells wafting from Beeji's kitchen, and other little things could bring uncomplicated joy. When there were no unanswered questions, no mind-numbing loneliness, no smouldering anger and no excruciating pain in her heart. Had there ever been a time when that was the case? She wiped the tears that had begun to flow.

Subodh poured oil in the lamps, Sumita began arranging the *puja thali* and Beeji laid out the idols. The rituals and actions performed year after year surfaced in Anya's mind, emerging fuzzy from deep within the shadows. The stage was set for a ritual that Zoya had loved, and one that she would never be a part of again. Anya dipped into Subodh's pocket and covered her head with his handkerchief—for as long as she could recall, when Subodh would come for the Diwali rituals, his pockets would be bulging with spare handkerchiefs for both his daughters.

All of them were silent for a moment, as the sadness and grief which had taken a permanent residence in their hearts made space for prayer, if not hope or joy. The anger and helpless rage in their minds were quelled, however briefly, by a feeling of surrender. A few fragile moments where the familiar motions of the body brought stillness to their hearts.

Beeji took the lead, as she always did, from the low pouf stool. Despite the sadness, there was a comforting familiarity to the rituals. They concluded with the hymn for Goddess Lakshmi which they sang in chorus—Subodh's deep baritone in perfect sync with Sumita's soft voice, both unwavering. Then, each one took an extra, wordless moment. They were all remembering Zoya. Anya saw a tear drop from her mother's eye when she helped her grandmother get up from the pouf. And saw how Beeji pulled her closer and wiped the tear away. "Sumita, be strong." Anya looked away.

"Let us get going for Gurgaon. We must not get too late." Subodh broke the silence. "Everything is already in the car. We can leave in 10 minutes." Anya called out, grateful for having something to do.

"Anya, will you help me with my things please?" Beeji called out.

"Sure Beeji, coming."

"Papa, can I take the other car? I might want to catch up with a friend later."

"Sure. Why don't you take Beeji with you? Sumita and I will follow."

Driving out onto the highway, Anya looked forward to Neel's company. Tonight would be especially difficult. She needed to keep herself from thinking about how, as little kids, Zoya and she would sample sweets and burst firecrackers. And how, just two years ago, Anya, Zoya and Laura had sat on the terrace chatting late into the night. Anya had looked at the two of them—Zoya's head had rested on Laura's shoulder and Laura had kissed Zoya tenderly on the forehead. Both were so obviously in love with each other that Anya had felt overwhelmed with joy for her sister.

'Serenade Villas', a neon sign announced. It was a charming neighbourhood. The wide amaltas lined roads were a contrast from the congested approach to their home in Old Delhi. Anya pulled over and helped Beeji out of the car. "It is beautiful, isn't it?" Beeji asked.

There was no doubt that the two-floor villa, with its landscaped garden was beautiful. Beautiful just like so many places were. But Anya couldn't bring herself to feel anything about it—excited, happy, or even anger. It didn't feel like it was hers. It didn't feel like home.

Beeji felt the pain in her silence.

"Anya, we make a house a home. Our moving out of the old house does not change anything. The house is part of your memories and will always remain so. But your memories do not reside in the house; they live in your heart, and your soul. Nothing can take them away from you. Even if we become frail and forgetful, like your grandfather did, those memories and experiences have become a part of you."

They had all heard how Beeji had lovingly cared for her husband who had struggled with dementia for two of the six decades he had lived. Anya took Beeji's tiny hands in hers and led her to driveway where Subodh had just pulled up. They would all go inside together.

Anya helped Beeji set up the Ganesh and Lakshmi idols which they had brought. She saw Subodh put his arms around Sumita's shoulders and Sumita clasp his hand. She sat cross legged on the floor next to her parents. She looked at Beeji sitting on the single plastic chair, her hands gently pressing on her aching knees, and felt an enormous tenderness for her loving grandmother. With nothing around them in this new house—no furniture, no items to announce belonging and possession—it was just the four of them. A family bound by pain, sorrow, happiness, dreams, memories, love, understanding and acceptance—as only family can be. When they had walked in an hour earlier, this large empty living space had felt like a huge void. Now, the void felt a little smaller. Less fearsome. Just like it had earlier this evening, the darkness seemed to shift a bit. A tiny bit, but a bit, nonetheless. Could this house also begin to feel like home? Could her memories find shelter here? She shrugged. It might be possible, but it didn't feel probable.

She went through the motions of the rituals again.

Anya quickly checked her messages.

Neel had shared the location of his house.

"Papa, I am meeting Neel. I will see you at home later."

"Bye, love."

Roy dropped a picture of the Diwali celebrations in the prayer hall of the hospital. As she drove on, she hoped that Roy wasn't as stressed as he had been the last few days.

18

Being One-Up

At his home, Neel watched his parents prepare for whatever little rituals Praveen and Lata followed. The Diwali ceremony at their home had always been a brief affair. Like every year, Praveen took out the clay idols from their usual place on a shelf in the library, where they shared space with the ultimate manifestation of the Almighty—knowledge. While they never professed to be atheists or even agnostic, his parents were pragmatic and commonsensical. They believed that work was worship and practiced learning with the faith that most people showed towards religion.

Praveen gently draped a string of white flowers on the large bun that Lata had knotted her thick waist length hair into. Lata handed over the *thali* to Praveen and Neel watched the long slender fingers of the surgeon shelter the flame before he kept it on the table and reach for his camera.

"Praveen, try the p-654 lens that is best for close ups."

"Lata, the r-9876 is better."

This was how Neel always remembered his parents' conversations—because this is how Praveen and Lata were. They were overachievers and perfectionists. They excelled at everything—even at outdoing each other. As a child he had thought that these conversations were more like confrontations, but at this moment, they seemed to be completely in sync with each other.

Praveen and Lata had been classmates in their medical college. Both had been outstanding and ambitious students. They had competed for the first spot and gold medals all through the MBBS course. When they had completed their training to become doctors, they had also decided to get married.

Praveen decided to train as a neurosurgeon. The brain was the final frontier which controlled personality, emotion, memory, language, and movement. It was one of the most arduous areas of specialisation.

Lata elected to study anatomy and cell biology. She would unravel the mysteries that the cell carried within it. It was something that needed a lot of tenacity along with a strong scientific temperament.

Three decades later, both were luminaries in medicine. They also continued to compete in whatever they could. Their spirit and love hadn't died down with time. Their accomplishments, their powerhouse personalities and their illustrious careers never failed to make feel Neel inadequate. How disappointing it must have been for them to have a son who floundered in his studies and career!

Neel watched as Praveen captured the flickering flame of the oil lamp, then trained his camera on Lata who was looking resplendent in a red and gold silk saree and traditional jewellery. It was a departure from her usual functional look of South cottons salwar kameez sets or formal trousers.

Right now, it felt very different from how Neel had always remembered their lives and home to be. For doctors, training, studying, examinations, and certifications move parallel with other life milestones like starting a family. That was how it had been for his brilliant parents in those early days as they eked out their career paths. Maybe that was why Neel remembered home as a place where he felt alone when his parents were at work, and lonely even when they were with him. He craved their time, attention and approval. Always. And he believed that he wasn't getting it because he wasn't good enough. That they wanted him to be perfect...like them. And he just wasn't. Having larger than life influences had made him believe he couldn't live up to the examples they had set. Now, it felt like he was seeing them—and his life—with a new set of lenses. One that wasn't coloured with his assumptions. Because whenever he looked back upon his childhood and adolescence, he couldn't remember his parents having demanded that from him. Had he put those expectations and those benchmarks for himself? Why had he done it? Was it because he was afraid of failure? And wasn't it easier to blame his parents rather than facing up and taking responsibility for his not being as successful or intelligent as them?

The sound of Lata's melodious rendition of the hymns filled the room. Lata's singing, rare though it was, was one of the most abiding memories of Neel's childhood. He loved the lullabies, the hymns and even the Happy Birthday songs she sang for him. Praveen was completely immersed in his wife's beautiful voice, singing along softly, as if not to dilute the beauty that Lata was bringing to the high-pitched song. Neel felt a calmness that had evaded him for long. He hoped that it would also help him take the decision he had been pondering about. For now, he was looking forward to exchanging notes with Anya.

"You will join us for dinner, won't you?" Praveen said as he neatly sliced the green chillies and coriander for the special dinner which Neel had helped Lata prepare.

"Sure." Neel replied, and realised that, unlike earlier, he was also looking forward to dinner with his parents.

"Where to?" Anya tapped the steering wheel impatiently.

"Let's drive down the Golf Course Road. And then go towards Cyber Hub."

They chatted as they drove, taking in the newly done up roads, underpasses and flyovers. The tall glass buildings were lit up. Intricately draped lights glittered on tree trunks and along the roads. Neel pointed out a few of the landmarks to Anya.

"Let's pull over for some coffee?"

The winter chill was yet to set in, and the evening breeze was just right. One of the few shops still open in a roadside market was a tiny kiosk with an old-fashioned coffee machine, not the modern-day types which were seen in coffee outlet chains.

Neel chatted briefly with the elderly lady who generously sprinkled drinking chocolate powder on the froth before handing then the Styrofoam cups.

Neel and Anya walked back to the car.

"Let's call and check on Roy. He seems to have been busy with the work on the maternity wing." Anya suggested.

Neel nodded.

The hospital had been keeping Roy busy, but Neel, intuitive as ever, knew that there was more that was keeping Roy's heart heavy.

Neel video called Roy.

Roy answered on the first ring.

"What's up, buddy?"

"Been busy with meetings for the maternity wing. Hi! Anya, how is everything?"

"The interviews went off well. I uploaded the documents too."

The interviews were not what he was asking about.

Roy balanced the phone on the kitchen counter and opened a beer for himself. Anya's silk blouse shimmered in the dark of the car, and the charms of her flea market bracelets clattered as she sipped the coffee. Even in the dim light of the car, Roy could see the dark circles below her eyes.

The idea of arranging those interviews in the Diwali week had been planted in his head during one of their routine chats. Anya had been resolute about staying away from home and not wanting to celebrate the festival at all. Roy understood that for too long now, she had been trying to push the pain away. Now, the pain was pushing back; demanding to be felt. And in such a situation, he hoped, his gentle nudge would make a difference. Maybe finding herself back home for Diwali would loosen the tight knots of grief. He knew it would be intense, and difficult too. He hoped it hadn't been too much for her.

Neel thought Roy looked more than just physically tired; he seemed emotionally drained too. Even in their short friendship, he understood Roy well enough to realise that his friend was overworking himself deliberately to avoid thinking of the relationship which he sometimes alluded to, but never really talked freely about.

"So, are you taking up Naik's invitation of chess and beer?"

"Maybe."

Both knew that Roy was just saying it. He would spend the evening alone.

Roy was quick to change the topic.

"Neel, I need a favour. Could you pick up some granola bars from my place and bring them for me? Will need a lot of midnight snacks before the new wing gets inaugurated."

"Err, Roy I may extend my trip by a few days. My mom is constantly badgering me to attend a cousin's wedding." Even the blurry video couldn't hide the surprise on Roy's face. Neel attending family events was new!

"I could bring them for you," Anya said.

"Hey, I don't want to be a bother."

"You won't be."

Neel stood at the entrance of his home, silently soaking in the cloudless night. But today he didn't feel the urge to search for answers in the sky above. Because, within himself, he felt that something had shifted. Something inside him was telling him to have the conviction to follow his dream.

The sky was devoid of clouds, but Neel felt as if whatever he was always searching for was with him. There was something telling him not to hold himself back. To trust the universe and have the conviction to follow through on his dream. He smiled to himself and went inside.

As he climbed the stairs to his room, he could hear his parents discuss the newly launched medical studies curriculum, debating their views passionately. He smiled and logged onto his email account.

The emails had dropped yesterday, but he hadn't opened them. Last year too, he had filled these applications. But, when the results had been declared, he had not had the courage to check if he was selected or not. Always ambivalent and unsure of his choices, he had found refuge in not making one.

Now, with his inbox open on the screen in front of him, he paused.

He wanted this. Yet, he feared it. Going back to university, and finally pursuing the culinary course, was a leap of faith. He would need to overcome all the thoughts and fears that were limiting him.

He clicked on the email.

His application for the coveted Diploma in Culinary Arts at the Dehradun Culinary School, the highest ranked in India, had been accepted.

19

Earthen Lamps

Stillness and quietude had replaced the chaotic frenzy of the last few days. The honking of vehicles had been replaced by the sporadic bursts of firecrackers. Driving back home, Anya noticed a young girl, not yet in her teens, at a streetside stall. It was a stall selling earthen *diyas*. At a time when everyone was at their homes, this little girl was still selling her wares. The festival was over, and no one would need these anymore.

"Didi, please buy some. The festival comes only once a year."

"How much?"

'Five rupees for one. If you take a few, I can buy some sweets."

"Give me 50."

The child's smile was brighter than the lights on the houses. Her spirits buoyed by Anya's magnanimity; the girl continued to chatter as she carefully wrapped the *diyas* in a newspaper.

Anya reached for the box of sweets in her car.

"Happy Diwali, Didi. And thank you. I will share this with my sister who paints these *diyas*."

Anya felt a stab of pain. Of course, what could be better than to share sweets—and happiness—than with a sister.

While most of the houses she drove past were lit up, a significant few stood out because they weren't. Did they belong to those who had lost someone recently? How were they coping? Did they resent the spirit of celebration around them? How did they react when the people they met offered useless words of consolation like, "It's God's will"; "You will get over it"; "Time will make things better"? Did they feel like screaming with anger when they heard these phrases and sentences that were meaningless at best, insensitive at worst, and always inadequate? Like her, did they also swing from anger to acceptance to guilt to reconciliation within moments?

Anya drove through the city's centre—Connaught Place. The lights adorning the downed shutters and electric lanterns on the large white pillars made the usually bustling shopping area look beautifully serene. She stopped on a side and took a few pictures. Diwali evening was always a unique potpourri of smells, sights—and feelings. The little girl at the roadside stall had been right when she had softly said, "*Saal mein ek hi baar to aati hai* Diwali." Lights or no lights. Pain or happiness, either way, this was an evening that would come only once a year. Each Diwali—like time and life—would bring different things to different people. Happiness would gradually replace sorrow; and pain would shamelessly intrude on delightful times. When joy would come, the only certainty that it would bring with it would be of its finite nature. The profoundness of love would be matched by the depth of grief. Hope and uncertainty would ride in tandem. Darkness and light would be alter egos as much as opposites. Life would be peppered with disruptions, even upheavals. Yet, the sun and the moon, the seasons, and the festivals would remain constant, as they had done for centuries. A few months ago, she would have resented the world for going on; the Earth for spinning; and the seasons for their transition to one another. But right now, that consistency—and the sense of renewal of a new day, and a new season was reassuring, even if only for a moment.

Subodh had been waiting for Anya. He was glad that she had taken off to meet Neel. He had noted a change in her when she spoke about the new friends she had made in Goa. There was a lightness to her that he hadn't seen for very long. For those brief moments, it would be as if she was his chirpy, talkative daughter again. The one who always insisted on staying a kid forever. Until that transatlantic phone call that had changed everything. Sumita had agreed too. His wife had always been a quiet person, but their conversations were more and more one sided now—as if she were trying to drown her sadness in his words.

"Can I get you something to eat? There is some biryani for you."

"Hmm, sure."

She followed him into the kitchen. The biryani—a Delhi-6 speciality—was delicious. He watched Anya devour it.

20

Home Alone

Roy hadn't taken up Naik's invitation. Not in the mood to socialise, he had returned to his desk to finalise the inaugural event for the maternity wing. The event management firm had shared a proposal of a laser light show for the event, and he shared the video on the group. It would be good to know if Neel and Anya liked it. Besides, Anya was still in his thoughts. Just for a moment he wished that he had taken a short break and gone home for the festival too. Then he sternly reminded himself to avoid anything that could hurt him.

He waited to see if Anya had seen the video.

It had been a long day for Anya, but going to bed would rekindle memories she wouldn't be able to handle. The video of the laser show Roy shared was a welcome distraction.

"This is awesome!" Anya typed after seeing the video.

"The inauguration is going to be a big event." She added.

Anya was happy for Roy. She knew how deeply he desired to make the most of his self-imposed stint in hospital management. This maternity wing would be one of his major achievements. But she also knew that it wouldn't bring him the deep satisfaction that came from surgery. Surgery had his heart. He often called surgery his second love but remained tight lipped about his first relationship.

"Thanks for offering to bring my granola bars. Hope it won't be too much of a bother." Roy had texted.

Instead of replying, Anya called him.

"Hey!" Even though they had been on the group video call a while back, seeing her name flash on the screen gladdened his heart.

"The granola bars are no trouble, Roy." Anya started the conversation from what Roy had texted a few moments back.

Roy sometimes needed to remind himself that Anya was someone he had got to know only recently. They vibed well. He found it easy to laugh off his food preferences (issues, as Denise liked to call them) and granola bars with her.

"It's nice that you and Neel managed to catch up."

"Yeah, he has been a little secretive about something lately though."

"Yes, he sure is building up the suspense."

They chatted for a while about the hospital before hanging up.

Anya finally went to bed. She fell asleep without talking a sedative from the strip in her bedside drawer as she usually did.

21

Smog

When Neel woke up the next morning, the sky was a smoggy grey. He went downstairs. Praveen was fixing an old wall clock and Lata was reading a research paper.

"I was thinking of extending my vacation and doing a short road trip before I go back to Goa."

Lata browsed through the journal and waited for Neel to continue. It was unlike him to have come home for Diwali, and this sudden change in plan was unexpected too. She knew her son well enough to realise that pressing him for anything only made him unsure, so she kept her curiosity to herself.

"That's a good idea." Praveen said.

"Yes." Lata agreed.

"Hey, wait. Both of you agreed on something. I will need to post that on the internet to record it for posterity."

They all laughed.

Then Praveen turned towards Neel.

"Young man, why do you think we always disagree? Debating doesn't mean disagreement. In fact, even though you may not have realised it, we have always agreed with each other about important things. And the biggest thing that we agree upon is that we wish you find the happiness you are always searching for." Praveen said, softly.

Neel hadn't seen this coming.

"That is not true, Papa. Both of you always disagree on big things and small stuff alike."

Praveen waited. He knew there was more simmering under the surface.

"I was under so much pressure to follow in your footsteps and choose a career in medicine. It made me miserable. And, here you are, speaking of my happiness!"

Lata sighed. Their son always tried to read so much into everything. Suggesting a career in medicine had come naturally to them. But when in senior school Neel had said he didn't want to become a doctor, they had explored other options. However, Neel had not been receptive to any of those either. If he hadn't aced the swimming trials, he would not have even secured admission in the BCom course at a low-ranking university. He had never shown interest in furthering his education or career and believed that 'boredom' was a legitimate reason for quitting a job. And he was always bored, except when he was looking at his beloved clouds. She wished her son would find some stability and consistency in life. But for that, he first needed to take ownership of his life and his choices.

"Yes, we would have loved to see you become a doctor. But it was clear that you didn't feel similarly, and we understood that too. You became an accountant, but your heart wasn't in it. Over the years, we have seen you struggle, and that pains us. Because, my son, we want to see you happy and fulfilled. Your mom and I have always agreed that you must follow your heart. But to live your dream life, you must first articulate your dreams and work towards them. That is something no one else can do for you."

"For that, my dear Neel, you need to listen to your own voice first." Lata softly completed what Praveen was trying to explain.

Neel was startled. He had expected the usual lecture on the importance of a good career and climbing up the corporate ladder. Wrapping his head around this encouragement was not easy. He wished he could push the pause button on the thoughts swirling in his hand. Was it true that his parents were okay with his not becoming a doctor and not living up to their larger-than-life profiles? Had he assumed so much of what he now believed deeply? Not only had he not tried to make his dream of becoming a chef come true; he had given himself the ready and plausible excuse that his parents wouldn't approve of his career choice. Not trying was safer than failing, after all.

He had been miserable, but his parents hadn't been responsible for his misery, had they? Nor were they to blame for the trajectory of his life so far. During graduation, the BCom classes had been boring and tedious. Life in college would have been unbearable if he hadn't been the captain of the swimming team and prefect of the hostel mess. He had barely scraped through the degree exams and disregarded his parents' suggestions to become a Chartered Accountant. He had hoped finding a job would give him freedom from the drudgery of those classes. But he had continued to feel lost in the balance sheets and statements. Going to work had felt like a punishment and made him anxious and disturbed. Cooking for himself in his studio apartment had been the only time he felt alive. He wished he could cook for a living. Even as a child, he would love to watch Nina-ma cook in the kitchen while he played. He had been jealous of the beautiful kitchen set that girls were gifted routinely. His fascination with everything related to the kitchen had continued—the appliances, the cookware, and the seasonings. The sights and smells of the kitchen were as exciting as the energy and the vibe. Checking out cookbooks and cookery shows had become a pastime and then a passion. It was during college days that he first considered making it a vocation, but except on a rare occasion, he hadn't found the courage to bring it up with his parents. They had assumed the Sunday breakfasts that he fixed for them, and the checking out new restaurants and cuisines was merely a hobby.

His mother passed him a glass of juice. She was right; not listening to his heart had become the norm for him. It was the safer option and had served him well all these years. But now the restlessness had set in. Unfortunately, so had the inertia of being in his comfort zone. After all, years of habit didn't go away with just wishful thinking. He knew he had to break through the imaginary fence of self-doubts he had set up all around him. What if he finally listened to his heart and took the plunge to change the course of his career…only to fail at it?

Lata put her hand on her son's shoulder. "Sometimes, even though we deeply want something, we also stop ourselves from getting it. Maybe we feel scared that something will go wrong. Perhaps, we feel we don't deserve the happiness that it may bring us. Whatever the reasons, sometimes, finding the courage to claim our own lives is not easy."

How could a mother be so perceptive about her child's inner world? Also, how could she not?

"Neel, you shouldn't let the noise outside allow you to obscure your inner voice." Pravin said in his usual succinct style and returned to the wall clock, which he was now meticulously putting back together.

Neel assumed the conversation had been dismissed, but Praveen had something to add. "Neel, we will support you in whatever you really want and aspire to. Parents can wish their children the very best for their journeys, and they always do. We can be confidantes and cheerleaders; but it is the children who must walk alone. We believe in you. But do *you* believe in yourself?"

In that moment, Neel grew up little. He had always tried to read too much into his parents' discussions. They were both highly driven, intelligent people who didn't shy of expressing their strong views. They loved to compete—both with each other and with themselves. It was he who had interpreted this competition as conflict. More than their debates and banter, it was his own inner conflict that he was running away from. Was it really his parents who had stopped him from becoming a chef? He was the one who had never mustered the courage to try. Being evasive and dodging difficult situations had become a pattern. Could he begin to break free from these patterns now?

He decided to start by leaving for Dehradun the very next day to check out the campus and the course. Once he was sure of his decision, he would tell them everything.

22

Unboxing Memories

Anya's throat hurt when she woke up the next morning. When they were kids, the day after Diwali was marked by a chill in the air; a nip that was the harbinger of the approaching winter. Now, the concoction of emissions, smoke and dust would make itself felt. Anya sipped the tulsi tea Sumita had brewed and tried to prepare herself for what the day would bring.

Sorting out the things from the room Anya and Zoya had shared since childhood was going to be difficult. Anya's room in the new house was much bigger than the one there but it was a room she would never share with Zoya again. Since that fateful phone call, Anya had not slept here. Everyone had noticed how she had moved her things to the spare room downstairs. No one had commented.

She trembled as she forced herself to go upstairs.

Just outside her room, in the corridor, there was a wooden cabinet that contained keepsakes and memorabilia from the girls' growing up years—pictures from school events, prizes they had won, and even old toys. She averted her eyes.

"Anya, all those will go with us. I have designed a similar cabinet for these things there." Subodh, already in the room, saw her stop at the door.

He knew this wasn't going to be easy. Nothing was, anymore. There seemed to be no getting to the other side of the pain that had now become their reality.

Anya bit her lip.

"I don't know where to start, Papa."

"Let's try it this way, Anya. You can put the things into these boxes." Subodh began labelling the cartons which he had laid out as 'Keep', 'Don't keep', 'Maybe'. Anya stared absently at the bunk bed that she had shared with Zoya.

"I will be back in a bit."

Anya opened one of the wooden almirahs. It contained some magazines from their school and college days. There was a box with a lot of pebbles—the kind that were found on riverbeds. Smooth and grey, their edges weathered by the constant force of water, these had been keepsakes from their road trip to Manali when Zoya had been in the 10th grade. Zoya had painted a few of them in red and black like lady bugs. Anya clasped one of these lady bugs tightly in her hands. There was a tiny Taj Mahal replica that they had hidden away because Beeji said it would bring bad luck. Maybe it had. Anya could feel the flood of tears rising. These things belonged to both the sisters. How was she supposed to decide on Zoya's behalf? What if Zoya would have liked to keep something that Anya discarded? How could she even think of throwing things that Zoya had touched, knowing that that would never happen again?

There was a plastic pouch with metallic caps of soft drinks. Despite herself, Anya smiled. Collecting those caps, trading duplicate ones with friends, and racing others to be the first ones with a complete set had been a fad they had all enjoyed. There were books, files, folders, notes, bundles of question papers. She was beginning to feel overwhelmed at the many emotions this curious mix of things was giving rise to.

She started with the files and notebooks and dropped these into the 'don't keep' box. A worn and frayed backpack Anya had inherited after Zoya left for college. Anya hugged it close to her chest and recalled how she had carried that bag everywhere.

She dropped the bag in the 'maybe' box, then picked it up and moved it to 'keep'.

There were many more things. Some, like a set of Legos, were associated with vague memories. Others didn't make the memory wheels in her head churn at all—like a set of flash cards. And then there were things like the trinket box that Zoya had brought for Anya from a school excursion with both their names engraved, that threatened to send Anya into tears. There was an UNO card game which had rescued them from hours of boredom when Zoya had been seasick on a cruise. She would take it with her. It would be fun playing with Neel and Roy. Zoya's stethoscope—Keep. Forever.

When Subodh returned a few hours later, carrying a flask of ginger tea and hot samosas that Beeji had sent, the carton of 'Maybe' was overflowing.

Anya dipped the samosa into its gooey tamarind dip and then got back to the things strewn around them. Still wary of the memories, tears and misery that any of the objects could unleash, she inspected most of the items cursorily and continued making the maximum use of the 'Maybe' box. Subodh watched his lovely child struggle with this onerous task.

He thought to himself, *If only I could take some of your pain away, my dear daughter*.

"Do you want to take a walk?" he asked her.

They walked out of the house. The small lane on which they lived looked exactly the way it had when Anya was a toddler. The hyped restoration of this area had been limited to the main roads and had left the inner streets unchanged. Streets which contained as many memories as the house itself. Of the sisters enjoying the *Banta* soda—the quintessential, home-grown, marble pop drink of Old Delhi, with its lemon scented mist. Of the girls drawing the rectangle for hopscotch with coloured chalk and playing for hours. Of the makeshift badminton court that the roads were transformed into on weekends. Subodh waved at some of the families sitting in the small verandas or balconies, who acknowledged them too.

"Dad, won't you miss this place?"

"Yes, dear, I will. Like you, I have also spent my entire life here...my home, my work, my family—all of it has been here."

When he enrolled for the MBA course, Subodh had envisaged a high-flying corporate career. But his father's illness had pushed him into managing the family business. What he had thought was a temporary phase had gradually—and imperceptibly—become permanent.

It was during the course that he had met Sumita, who had studied fashion design and wanted to learn management to set up her own studio. The traditionally beautiful, fiercely independent Bengali girl and the soft spoken, handsome Punjabi boy had fallen quickly and deeply in love. The courtship ended with the course. Career and marriage had followed.

In his daughter's choice of a life partner, Sumita's father also found a buddy for the golf course. Sumita was welcomed by large hearted Beeji to their small home in the crowded lane of Chandni Chowk, which was filled with warmth and spontaneity of visits by friends and extended family. It was a complete departure from her childhood which had been spent in the structured environment of hostels because of her mother's multiple illnesses. And Sumita loved it. Without realising it, Sumita had traded the life she had planned to have for the one she was living. The years had passed, as they often do, both slowly and quickly. Life became quotidian, but was peppered with special events and developments. Some dreams had come true, others had been overshadowed by time and new developments had been embraced.

A gentle, assuring rhythm had developed to their days and nights, their months and years. Until the phone call that had shattered all of them.

Subodh wrapped his arm around Anya.

"Anya, once we move to Gurgaon, I want to be actively involved in your mother's design studio."

Anya was surprised. His business had always been at the forefront of his life. She couldn't imagine him devoting time to Sumita's work.

He registered her surprise. "Sumita always wanted to have her own fashion label. But it just didn't happen. Caring for you girls, Beeji's cancer treatment and helping me with my work took up all her time." His voice softened, but he continued. "It was Zoya who reminded me of this."

"But Mumma wasn't unhappy, Papa."

"No, I don't think she was unhappy. She did these because she wanted to. But maybe she could have been happier—or a different happy—if she had been able to realise her true potential. After all, she never got to live her dream."

"Neither did you."

"Yes, Anya, but these were my circumstances, my choices and compulsions which Sumita embraced. You know, once Zoya asked me if I would have done the same if the roles were reversed."

Anya knew the answer to that. Their father, who was ever so supportive of his daughters; whom they viewed as a staunch feminist had stopped short of applying the same principles of equality to his wife. Zoya—with her strong sense of right and wrong—had been the one to nudge him to this fact.

"Maybe this new design studio will help her heal a little."

"It would be good for you also, Papa." He nodded. A soft sigh accompanied his words. Sometimes the pain in his heart was so strong that he felt it would make the life ebb out of him.

They walked back home in silence, where the three cartons awaited them.

"There are so many textbooks. These might be useful for you."

"Papa, most are outdated editions, and we have newer versions available online. Anyway, let me check for something that may be useful later."

She perfunctorily went over the books, opening a few just to relive the feeling of medical school. A few dried flowers fell out of a surgery textbook. Before she could pick them up, Subodh had put them tenderly in his shirt pocket.

"Zoya used to love doing this. She would use them to make cards."

"Yes, but what are you going to do with them?"

"He will put them away in that zip lock bag of his, where he has kept Zoya's school ID card, her scribbled musings, and some of her hand-made cards. He keeps it under his pillow."

Anya turned to see Sumita standing at the door. Tears were flowing down her mother's cheeks, as she joined them on the floor.

They sat there in a huddle—the three of them, and their grief, for a while. Then they composed themselves. Maybe this task would be easier if they did it together. In tacit agreement, they worked in silence. Words were dangerous because they could start an avalanche of grief.

A few photo albums—those slim ones with plastic pockets slots. Keep, of course. A box of trinkets. Discard. Pencil cases with stubs of colour pencils. Colouring books. Anya broke the silence. "Do you remember how weird it was when Zoya began colouring as a hobby?"

"Yes, I thought that was for kindergarten kids; and here she was, entering college and stocking up on pencils and sharpeners." Sumita agreed.

The academic pressures of first year of college had been very difficult for her introverted elder daughter. Zoya had taken to colouring as a stress buster.

Subodh could feel Anya's eyes on him, as he dropped the pencils in the 'don't keep' carton.

He took her hand in his.

"Anya, Zoya lives on in us. In our hearts and souls. Nothing can diminish those memories...not even discarding some of these things. Yes, sometimes, these things, or pictures help us to relive those moments she spent with us. But those moments have also touched us deep within. Keep whatever you wish to always have a bit of Zoya with you. But don't feel guilty over not keeping any item, either."

Anya nodded. Just yesterday, Beeji had said the same thing in the context of moving to the new home. It sounded simple but didn't feel easy at all.

They had managed to clear most of the cupboards by evening.

'I will go and help Beeji with dinner. She gave all the helpers an extra day off, and now wants to prepare her special mutton curry for you." Sumita hugged Anya.

"I also have a couple of calls to return."

Subodh shut the door behind him. How he wished closure could be like the definite, final click sound that closing the door made. But was that even possible? Did closure even exist? No one knew what closure felt like, did they? Yet, everyone kept searching for it.

Anya sorted out the remaining few articles and then sat on the lower bunk of the bed. When sleep would elude Anya, she would climb up and cuddle up to Zoya. The girls would keep chatting with each other even after they switched the lights out. When Zoya left for college, Anya missed her terribly and she would climb up to the upper bunk and sleep there, finding comfort in Zoya's soft cushions. Later, it remained Zoya's happy place where she would disappear whenever she wanted some time and space to herself, often writing or doodling in one of the many journals she had kept.

Anya reached into the 'keep' carton for Zoya's diaries she had found and carried them downstairs with her.

Beeji's mutton curry could put the fanciest chefs to shame.

"What time do we need to leave for the Govardhan puja at the studio tomorrow?" Sumita asked Subodh. It was the annual ritual where craftsmen and workers paid reverence to their tools.

"Around 11."

"Dad, I could also come with you. I need to pick up some things from Roy's home."

After dinner, Anya lingered in the courtyard. Being home for Diwali had been difficult. But she didn't regret the trip. These would be the last memories they would all have of this home, neighbourhood and life as they had known it. These memories were to be cherished too, just like the memories of Zoya which she now found herself coming back to. Of course, she had missed Zoya. But being with her parents and Beeji had brought her—and them too—some respite from their sadness.

The message notification pinged.

"Dad will have the snack bars ready and packed in the morning."

Once again, she called back instead of texting.

"Perfect."

And suddenly, just like that, she found herself sharing little vignettes of her life with Roy. Snippets about growing up, her days from school and college, idolising Zoya, her training in medicine. About random moments from their lives. Everything. Nothing.

Roy listened. He had heard some of these before. But what was different was the lightness with which she spoke. Especially about Zoya. Today she didn't clam up at the smallest mention of her beloved sister, or her home, or family. A weight had been lifted, even if it was for a few moments.

From their room, Subodh and Sumita watched their daughter laugh as she spoke on the phone. They couldn't hear the spontaneous conversation, but they could see her face. She looked like their effervescent daughter again—the one that had got lost in a maze of grief and sorrow. The one they missed as much as the daughter they had lost to a bullet from the gun of a shooter consumed with hatred.

It was midnight when Anya and Roy were done talking. Anya returned upstairs to the 'Maybe' carton. There were a lot of things in it which she was now able to put in the 'Don't keep' carton. Then, instead of returning downstairs, she slept in the room she had shared with her dear sister all her life.

23

First Love

The skyline of Gurgaon had a different, but equally imposing feel to it in the daylight. Subodh drove past the towering facades towards the alcove that led to their new home. All of them were thinking the same thought—that Zoya would have loved it when the yellow-green blooms would carpet the paths in summer.

"Dad, I will pick up the things from Roy's house and meet you in a while."

"Sure."

Anya pulled up at the address Roy had shared.

"Welcome. I am Radha."

Anya followed Roy's mother into an elegant living room done up in minimalistic light blue. A large oil painting occupied one entire wall. It was a water colour of a mountain scenery where the flame red vibrancy of the gulmohars blended harmoniously with the greys of a winding street. Anya was captivated—it looked so much like the paintings of professional artists she had seen with Roy in the gallery in Goa. It must be expensive, she thought. Then she noted the initial at the bottom corner. 'Radha' written in a stylised blend of Roman and Devanagari scripts.

Roy's father, Raman, who was wearing a kitchen apron over his polo t-shirt and denims waved to her from the open kitchen behind the living space.

"Would you like some cranberry crush? I made it while I was drying cranberries for Roy's energy bars."

The delicate, sweet taste of cranberries in the bubbly soda was delicious.

"So how is everything at the hospital? Roy seems to have his hands full with work." Radha asked.

"Yes, the maternity wing project is keeping him busy."

"He always does take on more than he can handle." Radha smiled.

"But then, Radha, he always manages to pull it off, doesn't he?" Raman laughed.

"I was worried that being away from surgery and taking up the desk job would be frustrating for him. I hope he isn't unhappy." There was a question in Radha's words. A question that Anya didn't have the answer to. Roy kept his feelings close to his chest. If he was unhappy, he hadn't mentioned it. But then again, she had seen how he was in his element when he was wielding the scalpel. She couldn't imagine him being happy in his desk job.

Anya realised Radha was waiting for her to reply. "He is doing a wonderful job."

Radha smiled—a tender smile filled with pride and love; that lit up her face. And a smile that was exactly like Roy's when he had spoken about his mother's artistic talent.

"Roy mentioned that your new home is not far from here." Raman said.

"Yes, it's called Serenade Villas. I am not very familiar with Gurgaon though."

"You will love it here."

"When Raman gave up his job to be able to give more time to Roy, we had planned to live in Delhi. But Gurgaon had more open spaces—and some of the very best hospitals too. With Roy's food allergies and frequent hospitalisations, that was an important consideration."

"Radha, just because Anya is a doctor, it doesn't mean you bore her with talk of illness." Anya noted how, just like Roy, Raman quickly deflected any mention of Roy's health issues.

"Come, let me show you my workplace." Anya followed Raman into the kitchen. Jars containing nuts, dried berries, oats and other condiments were lined up. Chopping boards, knife sets, and kitchen scales completed the MasterChef look. It was difficult to be untouched by Raman's enthusiasm as he shared some of his signature recipes with her.

"Raman became interested in cooking when Roy was little." Radha explained.

"I didn't have a choice. His complex allergies meant that his food choices needed to carefully be thought out. Any wrong choice could leave him writhing in pain. Even the doctors were out of their depth when it came to understanding Roy's case. I kept a diary and painstakingly recorded the ingredients in whatever Roy ate, and how his body reacted to them. If Roy's diet needed to be customised, it was best done by me."

Confronting Roy's illness had been a watershed event for Raman. At that time, he had been a young man on the exciting thresholds of family and career. The unexpected situation, and how helpless he was in the face of Roy's illness, had been difficult to accept. Having never been one to be a victim of circumstances, he had responded by taking bold decisions. He had quit his new job in the Indian Foreign Services and decided to devote himself to Roy's health. Taking charge of the situation was his antidote to frustration. It was also a defence from the mixture of guilt, sorrow and anguish of a parent.

Anya saw the fresh bars that Raman had been preparing for Roy. These were labours of love, which could come only from a parent.

"Anya, Roy called in the morning He needs some books. Let me forward his message to you." Radha reached for her phone.

Anya checked the list. They were mostly surgery textbooks, which meant that Roy was thinking about getting back to surgery. She wondered if she too should apply for her training in the US again; then pushed the thought away. As always, she had wanted to follow in

Zoya's footsteps. But there was no compelling reason for her to go to the US anymore.

"Why don't I take you up to Roy's room? You can pick out the books he wants." Radha said and broke Anya's train of thoughts.

"Sure."

The staircase led to a landing with a large work bench and a computer behind which hung a huge art canvas. It was another water colour—a beautiful rendering of the Japanese cherry blossoms painted by Radha.

Anya was taken in by its beauty.

"You are such a phenomenal artist."

Radha corrected her. "*Was* an artist, my dear. I don't paint anymore."

Behind the computer table Anya caught a glimpse of a folded easel.

Roy's room was done up in the Manchester United colour scheme. Anya knew he was an ardent fan of football and keenly followed the Goa Professional League too. But it was when she saw the cabinet full of trophies, cups and medals that she realised he was an experienced player too.

Radha sat on the bed and waited for Anya to check out the many mementoes from Roy's football days.

"When Roy gave up football, he would tell me to put his medals and trophies away. But despite his pleas that his tryst with football was over, that he would never be reunited with his first love again, I couldn't bring myself to do it. Even if he couldn't play football anymore, it would always remain a part of him. So, we pretended that this cabinet was for me; that he was humouring me by agreeing. But I know that in those difficult days and terrible nights, these gave him strength. Strength to accept and finally move on."

"I didn't realise he was such a good player," Anya said, quietly.

"The Under-17's was a dream come true. Until they weren't."

"Under-17?"

"Under-17 Nationals. They could have been his gateway to a professional career."

Radha pointed to a framed news piece mounted on cardboard. It was a picture of Roy with Baichung Bhutia. The headline read: 'Gurgaon boy makes it U-17 Nationals; Bhutia sees potential'.

"Roy played in the nationals?"

"No, he never got around to it. In one of the training matches he had a knee ligament tear which needed surgery. The recovery would be long, and there was no certainty that he would be able to play as well as before, if at all. From his childhood, he had nurtured one ambition—to be a football player. That was what had sustained him through the bouts of his illness. Being on the field, out there, immersed in the game, was the only time he ever forgot his illness."

Anya took all this in slowly. What she had taken to be a fancy for the sport was a passion. And a broken dream too. It must have hurt terribly. Yet, Roy had never spoken about it.

"Those two years were the worst we could imagine. He became withdrawn. And then, he went on a self-destruct mode. That was easy for him. All he needed to do was eat normal food. He would hang out with friends, eat pizza, binge on burgers at birthday parties and fall sick the next day. It took us some time to figure out that it was subconscious. He was inflicting physical pain on himself so he could forget his grief." Radha continued.

"But he is so careful now about what he eats. I could never tell that he has this issue."

"He has to be. He almost died once after one of those episodes. Something he had with his friends triggered an intense allergy. His kidneys shut down, and he was on life support for a while. We made him swear he wouldn't take such risks ever again. Once Roy was out of hospital, his melancholy remained. He felt that if he couldn't become a football player, life wasn't worth living. We were so worried he would try and harm himself."

"But he became a doctor."

"Yes, that decision was a surprise for us too."

"He must have been inspired by the doctors he met in his hospital visits?"

"Partly yes. But it was also because becoming a trauma surgeon had a few things in common with being a football player."

Radha noted Anya's surprise and explained. "Roy wanted action. Fast stuff. He needed to do something where his reflexes, razor sharp as they had become with his football training, could be put to use. For him, the time spent on the football field had been a meditative experience, where nothing except for him and the ball existed. He could forget every other thing in his life and just focus on his shots. In surgery, he found a parallel. It was just him and the patient; and he needed to act fast and with great skill. His precision, judgement and confidence would affect the outcome totally."

It was beginning to make sense to Anya. So, it was football that had been his first love. Roy had worked so hard to succeed in football—only to have it snatched away from him. It must have hurt. It probably still hurt, she corrected herself. Training in medicine was not easy, and he must have worked hard with a vengeance for his career in surgery. He had given his frustration a direction; invested enough of himself in it to call it his second love. And then he distanced himself from surgery. She could almost feel his pain at whatever had made him do that.

Radha didn't know why she was having this conversation with Anya; someone she had never met before. Maybe it was easier to talk to a stranger. Not expressing feelings had been normalised in their home decades ago, because Raman believed on focussing on the positive; on doing things instead of talking about them and 'moping around'. Raman always laughed away those difficult days. His sunny disposition and spirited nature had been a huge blessing, but sometimes it also made it difficult for her to voice her inner thoughts. Sharing her angst or sadness made her feel guilty for not appreciating Raman enough. Raman had given up so much for their family. He was like a saint. And being married to a saint was not easy.

"It must all have been so difficult." Anya asked, sensing Radha's thoughts.

"Roy's infancy was a difficult phase," Radha agreed. "We were a young couple building careers and raising a family. Suddenly, we found ourselves in and out of hospitals. All our time, energy and money were consumed. We were unable to find any method in the madness. Finally, Raman quit his job. It was an unconventional decision. But one of us needed to be there." Radha tried to keep her voice neutral.

"You gave up so much too."

"Not really, I had my job. And the accolades that came with a successful career in the Revenue Services."

And the guilt of going to work leaving a sick child at home, Radha added to herself.

"But you gave up art."

"That was nothing to what Raman gave up," Radha replied tersely.

Radha paused for a moment to keep the bitterness out of her voice.

"I mean, with Raman leaving his job, one of us needed to maintain financial stability so I continued working."

This was true. But was it the only truth? There was no denying that Raman's decision of becoming a 'Stay at Home Dad', however impulsive it had been, had been good for Roy. It was a bold step—audacious, even when you considered societal convention. But that was how Raman did everything in life—with a lot of confidence and conviction. The same conviction that had attracted her to him in college, even though she was a teacher and he a student. 'No half measures for Raman Bhaskar' was a phrase that he repeated often. And that was a dictum he followed in everything—his studies where he excelled, ranking very high in the UPSC exams, his relationship with her and their family. Submitting his resignation so that he would have time to attend to Roy was another example. It was also an irrevocable step that would affect their lives in many ways. Yet, he hadn't even discussed it with her. The night she had returned from an outstation trip was etched in her mind. Roy was in the ICU after a severe bout of allergy, and Raman was sitting beside him, stroking his son's hair. "I quit," was all he had said. The meaning and magnitude of those words had taken time to sink in. Decades later, Radha still wondered what turn their lives—hers especially—would have taken if things had been different that night. If she hadn't gone for her training. If she had been the one staying the night in the hospital with Roy. If she had given up her career to raise her child, and nurtured her love for art. The hurt of not being asked, not having been given a chance to participate in the decision had died down. But sometimes these doubts, these many 'ifs' came to the fore again—a reminder that not all that looks fixed has healed.

Sometimes, in those dark nights, after long workdays, when she sat at Roy's bedside, she would agree that Raman's decision made sense. She had already invested a lot of herself in those early tedious tenures that came with the job. Raman, on the other hand, had just started out. But on days when she needed to be at work while Roy needed to go through the rigmarole of tests and scans and endoscopies, she would be very angry with Raman. The role reversal which had taken place had been his decision. Not hers. It didn't feel fair to be away when all she wanted to do was hold her son close to her. But, to say this would have felt like an injustice to Raman, who had given up everything. Like Roy's football aspirations, she too had nurtured a dream. Of paints and canvas and colour and creativity. Of working for a few years and then becoming a full-time artist. Her sacrificing her dream had been eclipsed by his giving up his career. She had never spoken about her unfulfilled dream; but she had not forgotten it either. What she had lost might have been trivial in the face of what they as a family had gone through. But did it matter if what she had lost was small or big? Was there some kind of a scale that measured loss and attached a magnitude of sorrow that could be felt for a particular loss? Did it matter if the loss one experienced was of a person, a dream, a thing or a desire? All loss came with pain and left a void; and each of us felt loss differently.

Over the years, they had got to get a grip on Roy's illness. Raman was excellent at everything he chose—managing the home and caring for Roy included. Radha excelled at her job in the Indian Revenue Services. Roy had put so much behind him to become a good surgeon. The unfairness of life, as it often does, became something less to be talked about and more to be walked through. Life wasn't supposed to give you everything you had wanted, was it? And for Radha, even thinking about wanting anything more than what she had seemed like travesty. A son whose life was a miracle, a wonderful husband, a good career—would it not be ungrateful to ask for more? When Roy had sent her those art supplies, she had put the box away, with the easel which had not been unfolded for years. But the thoughts had been unfurled.

Anya looked at Radha, who was lost in her thoughts. "Roy really loves you," she said, softly.

That was another thing Radha had feared. With Raman so devoted to Roy; always being available for him, caring for him—would Roy love her less? It was a fear that was rooted in the guilt that is birthed in a woman even before her child. Of course, Roy's love for her was as deep as his love for Raman, and she knew it. But in those days when she would be away from her, the question would crop up in her mind often enough.

Enough about herself, Radha thought and changed the topic.

"So, your mother is setting up a design studio?"

"Yes, she always wanted to do that. But you know how moms are. They always keep putting their dreams on the back burner for their families."

Radha smiled. "You children make everything worth it! Join me downstairs when you are done with the books."

Radha shut the door behind her.

Sitting in Roy's house, chatting with his parents about politics and cranberries and football and hospitals, looking at his collection of trophies, Anya felt she understood Roy much more than before. He had not allowed his allergies to define him. His illness was his story, but not his only story. Roy had successfully channelled his anger into determination.

When she left the room with the books, the easel was opened out, and the box of paints that Roy had bought from the art gallery lay next to it. But Anya was so wrapped up in thoughts of Roy that she didn't notice any of this.

24

Sunshine

Goa was a sunny balm after the pollution laden air of Delhi.

In the cab, she caught up on her messages. And with her friends.

"Hey, you have been MIA."

Neel had replied to Roy. "Busy with the wedding shenanigans."

"Must be a pain."

"It's ok, actually. Fun, even."

She couldn't help raising her eyebrows. Neel enjoying family events was not something she could imagine.

"No pictures?" Roy had caught on to Neel's bluff too.

Neel not sharing picture by picture accounts of everything was not like him at all. Even his Instagram feed had been silent.

In response, Neel had sent a picture of a chicken crossing the road.

"Neel, if you don't send us a picture of you, we will assume you are getting married secretly."

He replied promptly with a picture. Of a deep blue sky that was clear except for a single wispy cloud.

Anya laughed and rolled down the window to take in the breeze.

There would be time for a quick walk along the beach before her night shift. Maybe Roy would join her, she thought.

Roy had left a bag of groceries outside her apartment.

"Thanks for the goody bag. Next time, add some chocolates." She texted him.

The phone rang as soon as the read notification appeared. "Hey. You want chocolate after gorging on all those delicious Diwali sweets in Delhi?" Roy pretended to sound indignant. She laughed.

"Busy day?' she asked.

"Sort of. Should be done in an hour."

"Want to catch up? We could walk to the beach before I leave for my night shift."

"Sure. We could also have dinner at one of the shacks."

"Perfect."

"It is purely selfish of me. I know you won't have a drink before your shift starts. So, I will get to have all the beer." Roy laughed.

"That is clever. I won't give you your granola bars if you don't stop laughing."

"Ha. What would you do with them, then? There is not another single person for whom those bars would mean anything."

In his head, Roy could hear Denise rant, *"It is so frustrating to be with you, Roy. There is no spontaneity in our relationship. Everything is decided by your food. And those granola bars that you carry around everywhere—so embarrassing."*

Meanwhile, Anya wondered, *How does he manage to joke about himself, without showing any bitterness?* The suffering he had undergone as a young child was behind Roy's inherent empathy and kindness. Yet, he always hid his sensitivity behind this light veil of humour.

25

Back at the Beach

Anya was waiting for Roy outside the hospital gate. They walked to the beach. Roy took off his shoes and socks and rolled up his trousers up to his knees. Anya left her Crocs there too, and they walked barefoot in the sand, enjoying the water tickle their toes; leave some sand on their feet, then wash it away. Roy stopped to pick up a large seashell, pearly and translucent that reflected the orange of the setting sun and dropped it in his pocket. The shacks were lit up and bustling with the chatter of tourists. Strains of music wafted towards them. Roy gently slid his hand into Anya's. Her heart skipped a beat.

They walked towards one of the beachfront shacks. The music was soft enough not to drown the sounds of the ocean and the rays of the setting sun filtered through the clouds. The colours of the sky were mirrored on the waves below. Anya loved how the receding orange ball and the kaleidoscopic hues of the horizon were the build-up to the single moment when the sun finally set. It was a magical moment which you could miss even if you had been waiting for the sunset for hours. And she hated missing it. Her attention focussed on capturing the sunset, she absently tapped her feet to the instrumental music playing. She undid the scarf that she had used to try and keep her hair in place, and let her hair fall loose, framing her face. Roy's heart skipped a beat.

"So, what do you want to eat?" Anya asked. The moment was over in a flash. The sun was no longer in the sky and Roy's self-doubt was back as soon as Anya asked this innocuous question.

He could hear Denise in his head again. *"It is so difficult being with you, Roy. It's all about you—where we will go, what we will do, what we will eat—all about you."*

"You go first, Anya. I will figure later."

"A large grilled pomfret."

Her foodi-ness usually made him smile, but not today.

"A beer and a green salad."

"Not even ice cream?"

"No, I am good. I will raid my special refrigerator once I get home."

Again, the humour, Anya thought to herself.

Again, the voice in his head: *"Everything about you is special, individualised. Going out with you is both frustrating and embarrassing. You are so selfish, Roy, always thinking only of yourself."* The mockery had hurt. The hurt lingered.

Roy steered his thoughts away from the past. He didn't want anything to spoil this evening. Anya chatted as she devoured the fish—mostly about the crowded airport and Delhi's pollution; he listened.

"Neel still hasn't let on about what's going on with him." Anya complained.

It was fun to see Anya's patience getting tested by Neel's reticent behaviour.

Roy smiled. "Yes, he is being quite cagey about something. Let's wait and watch."

Anya grimaced. "I wish he wouldn't make us wait. I am dying to know what he is up to."

After the sky had changed colours from hues of orange to vibrant purples and the sun had disappeared completely, they walked back, chatting about the new wing of the hospital and Anya's new house in Gurgaon. They slipped their hands in each other's and headed back.

"It's time for my ER shift. Should I bring the granola bars over to office tomorrow?"

His eyebrows narrowed.

"Anya, I know people think I am weird, but can we at least not make it appear like I am an underworld cranberry granola bar trafficker?"

She giggled.

"You do have a polished gangsta vibe when you wear those pointy shoes."

Roy laughed. She never gave up on mocking him about those shoes.

"I discovered so many interesting ingredients of those energy bars—sultanas, figs, raisins. Your father gave me the whole tour."

"I keep telling dad to scale up and make it a business venture—Berries and Bars—he could call it."

"I loved your room. And your mother's art works were phenomenal."

Roy fell silent.

"Hey, what happened?"

"Err, nothing. Just tired, I guess," he managed.

"See you tomorrow then?"

"Yeah!"

Instead of going back to his apartment, Roy decided to go for a jog. He headed to the beach and began running at a steady pace, gradually increasing his efforts against the sand. Pushing himself had always been a coping mechanism for him. Today, he hoped that it would quell the voices in his head which had intruded on the lovely evening with Anya.

"You don't move on, Roy. Football is over. Why do you hang on to it in this pathetic way?"

"This room, Roy, it is a sign of everything that is wrong with you."

"Grow up, Roy."

Almost two years had passed since his breakup with Denise, but he still clearly recalled how their contempt had replaced caring in their conversations. The tone of her voice, and that word 'pathetic' often reverberated in his head—was that what she thought of him? Was that what their lovely moments of togetherness had been reduced to? Roy could handle everything except for pity. *"I feel so sorry for you"*—the words had been the final nail in the coffin. He had opened himself only to Denise, and she had felt sorry for him. She didn't understand how he had gone through phases of struggle, surrender, and reconciliation; each one draining him at different points in time.

The breakup had him with a nagging and unrelenting incertitude about everything. He found himself unable to break the cycle of negative thoughts and self-depreciation.

Had the words stung so much because they contained a grain of truth? After all, his food allergies had consumed everyone's time and attention.

"It is only about you, Roy."

"Have you ever really done anything for anyone else? Given up something for someone?"

His father had given up his job, and his mother her dream of being an artist. Their lives had revolved around him—first his allergies, then his football and finally in supporting him when he trained as a doctor. And he, Roy, had never even realised how much his life was affecting everyone else. Maybe Denise was right. He was a selfish person, who didn't deserve a loving relationship. Since then, he had not wanted to come close to anyone. Letting people in gave them the chance to break his heart. The self-doubt had become insurmountable after the episode in the OR.

Outwardly he had moved on, but the voices in his head would return when he least expected or wanted them too. And today, these voices had also brought questions.

Anya had been in his room. What had she made of his broken dream? Had she also thought it was silly of him to keep his room decorated the way he did—as a reminder of the dream he had come so close to living?

What did Anya think of him? He hoped she wouldn't pity him. He wouldn't be able to take it if she did.

Despite the cool breeze, Roy was sweating. He stopped jogging and looked out into the sea ahead. In the darkness the blur of the ocean blended into the void of the sky. The waves seemed to hush themselves when they hit the shore, not disturbing the tranquillity of the beach. The lights from passing vessels could be seen in the distance—some twinkling, others blurred. It was a new-ish moon, waxing and incipient with a faint glow. But the stars sparkled. Roy didn't know much about constellations but there seemed to be some pattern these stars were forming. He felt sure that there was a pattern or shape to them—he just didn't know what it was. Sort of like life, maybe? He remembered what his mother had told him when he had been heartbroken after his knee ligament surgery: "Life always has a plan. Sometimes we don't know what it is. Still, we just need to have the belief, the faith and trust that it does. And that is enough to keep everything from crumbling." Maybe it was true. When he had taken up the position at Goa, Roy had been distraught. Now, he had begun to feel somewhat like his earlier self. His occasional forays to the OR had restored his confidence, and he had started filling applications for training in the US. He had found a good friend in Neel. And Anya, of course. With Anya, he found an understanding and a comfort that could be more than just friendship. But after so much emotional turmoil, it would be foolhardy to even entertain such thoughts.

When Roy walked back to his apartment a while later, the stars seemed brighter than they had been an hour ago.

He imagined Anya in his room, sitting against the red and yellow striped wall, reading the news clipping, looking for his textbooks. He felt a sense of relief that she knew about those parts of him that he wouldn't have been able to share of his own accord.

Anya's shift was busy and the only chance she got to check her messages was past midnight, over a quick tea break. Neel had been quite active on the group. And exasperating too. He had shared pictures—of roads and road signs. Thankfully there were no chickens in these ones; but she still couldn't figure what he was up to.

Roy had been silent on the group but had texted her on her personal window instead.

"Hope the ER wasn't too busy."

For Anya, this was an unlikely friendship. On the day of their orientation programme, Roy had irritated the guts out of her. But when they had started hanging out together she had realised she had been wrong about him.

He was very good at his work—both surgery and hospital management. And a nice person too. She felt understood and comfortable when she was with him—almost happy. But was happiness even possible anymore?

26

Pick Up

The next day when Roy rang her doorbell, he had a sports bag slung on his shoulder. And he was wearing football shorts too—a quick match after work, Anya guessed.

"Come on in."

"Coke or beer?"

"Err, Coke, and then beer?"

Anya laughed and went to get the cans of soda.

Roy looked around her room which was neat but also spartan. Her laptop was open at the website of the Montford University Hospital, Philadelphia—at the '*apply now*' page. Anya had mentioned that she had been applying for critical care fellowships in America some time ago. Though she had left the rest unsaid, Roy figured that she had shut herself to the idea after Zoya's death. Would Anya be able to summon the courage to start the application process again?

Lost in these thoughts, he almost stumbled over her suitcase. "I hate unpacking. Haven't even started yet." Anya apologised.

"I need to unpack as soon as I get back," Roy jibed.

"I could have guessed. You need things organised, like the hospital."

But that wasn't it. As a child Roy had spent much of his time in hospital wards in hospitals. Going back home and finally unpacking brought a sense of unparalleled relief to him. It meant, at least, a brief spell of time when he could have a normal life, like everyone else in his school.

Once more, he was reminded how difficult it could be for an onlooker to understand his unique circumstances.

Anya reached for her duffle bag and began handing out the nutrition bars that Raman had given her. Soon her bag was empty, except for Zoya's diaries which she had brought back with her. She quickly put them away. Not quick enough to miss the attention of a football player turned surgeon with razor sharp reflexes, though.

"It was nice meeting your parents," Anya said, *and seeing your room,* she thought.

He smiled, "Thanks! Yes, they are pretty amazing people."

"Yeah, parents are like that. Mine too."

"But Neel always avoids talking about his family. And his parents are such famous doctors."

"Hmm."

"Why is Neel always running away from them?"

"Is he?" Roy replied with a question.

"What do you mean?"

"I mean, is it them he is running away from? Or himself?"

Anya was silent for a moment.

"Have you never tried to get him to understand this, and to change?"

"Can I, Anya?"

"What?"

"Is it possible to get someone to change? Change is a journey which is dark, messy, uncomfortable and scary. And one which can lead you to the most unexpected of places. Would you undertake such a journey just because someone asked you to? The desire for change has to come from inside, not from someone or something outside."

Anya was thoughtful. Once, she had asked Zoya, if there was something that they could all do to make Beeji's sister from Canada have a change of heart. For Anya, it had been difficult to see Beeji suffer at the hands of her own sibling.

"We can't change someone, Anya. That is something that only they, themselves, can do. And they must really want it. The only person we can change is us." Zoya, patient, old soul as always, had said.

"Zoya would agree," Anya said softly and then corrected herself. "Would have agreed, I mean." The stab of pain that shot up whenever she had to mention Zoya in the past tense felt as painful as ever.

The tears prickling at the corner of her eyes were threatening to rush out.

Anya picked up the snow globe and handed it to Roy.

"That's her."

He looked at the picture of the two sisters laughing without a care in the world, and then at Anya trembling, struggling to keep her composure.

He hoped she was ready for this. He hoped he was ready for this.

"She was an obstetrician in the US. Just a few months into her gruelling residency, she took a vacation to Florida. She had just fallen in love, and the holiday was to be the start of a new phase in their relationship." Anya got the words out in a gush. "But some crazed youth with a deranged mind shot at the people sunbathing at the beach. She died on the way to the hospital."

Suddenly, Anya was sobbing like she never had before.

Roy pulled her close and held her. And he let her cry. There was nothing that he could do to take her pain away or lessen her suffering. Except being there for her.

A while later, the sobs subsided. Roy handed her a diet soda. She sipped it quietly.

"Want to head out somewhere?" Roy gently suggested. He hoped she wouldn't find it insensitive, given how upset she had been. But he intuitively felt that getting out would be good for her.

She nodded.

On Roy's bike, they drove through the inner streets of Goa. Roy stopped opposite a restaurant that they had frequented often. Anya followed him inside. The loud music left little scope for conversation; something which both were glad for. They just sat silently looking at the others revel in the music and strobe lighting, nibbling at their snacks.

"My turn to drive."

He passed her the bike keys. Riding pillion, he felt her body so close that he wanted to reach out and put his arms around her waist. He felt the tenuous, slender string of attachment between them that was more than friendship. But he resisted the temptation.

Roy dropped Anya at her room, picked up the granola bars and turned to leave.

"Roy."

"Huh?"

"Good night."

"Yeah."

Once again, he found himself wanting her.

"Anya..."

Impulsively, spontaneously and simultaneously, they came closer to each other. They touched each other, then hugged. And then, they kissed. It started as a tentative, gentle kiss but then, in a flash, it was something more assured, and then forceful. Once their tongues had explored each other's mouths to satisfaction, they remained standing there, close to each other for a few moments.

On the ride back home, the feel of the kiss lingered in Roy's whole being.

After Roy left, Anya lay on the bed, thinking about the evening. She, who always put up a brave front and hated making a scene, had broken down completely in Roy's presence. And she hadn't felt awkward or embarrassed. And then, she thought of the kiss, which had been one of the best ever.

Could Roy have feelings for her?

Did she have feelings for Roy?

Was she even capable of feelings anymore?

Back in his room, Roy berated himself for coming too close to Anya. How many times had he told himself that he didn't want to be in a relationship ever again. He just wasn't meant to find happiness, and even if he did, it would never last. He would only end up hurting himself and Anya if he allowed them to become anything more than the good friends they already were.

27

Dear Diary

It had been a very busy few weeks. Roy had been busy with the inauguration of the maternity wing, Anya in the training of ER paramedics. Neel had returned from Delhi a few days after Anya and was busy planning the opening of Grace's restaurant, which they were calling *Nimbus*. They still managed to hang out together. Neel, who continued being his secretive self, had also taken up swimming again. Anya and Roy would top off their rounds of Jenga with a walk on the beach. Sometimes, they would slip their hands in each other's or sit huddled close to each other in their favourite shack and watch the sun go down. But Roy never tried to kiss her again. If Anya noticed, she didn't show it either.

One day, after a beach barbeque, the trio sat at the beach. The ochre yellows of the setting sun had been replaced by inky blue and charcoal.

"I have a call with a vendor in London. I better get going." Roy finally broke the silence.

"It is getting late." Anya agreed. "Why don't we all head back?"

"Err, why don't you guys go ahead? I will come later."

Anya met Roy's eyes. This was typical of Neel these days. His preoccupied, pensive moods were frequent. Sometimes Anya wished she could shake Neel violently and ask him about what was weighing on his mind.

Roy simply shrugged. He was curious too, but not as impatient as Anya was. If Neel wanted to be left alone, it was fine by him.

"Okay. See you later."

Roy and Anya started walking back to the H-of-H campus.

"So, what now, Roy?"

"Huh?"

"I mean the maternity wing is done. And it's not like you not to have a huge mission. You need a project to keep you busy."

He laughed but didn't answer the question.

Anya let it pass. She had noticed how Roy always needed something that he could plunge into with all his energy and concentration. It was now clear that he was running away from something. But why? He was such a fabulous person, a genius at whatever he seemed to touch. He had gone through so much and had emerged stronger and more successful despite all the obstacles. Then what was it that he had not been able to rise above?

"Bye."

"See ya."

Back in her room, putting away her clothes in the wardrobe, Anya came across the diary she had kept there. *Zoya's diary.*

She sat with it in her lap, hands folded over it. She was torn between wanting to open it, and not having the guts to do so. When she had brought these diaries from Delhi, she had stashed them away. More than wanting to read them, she had just wanted to keep them close to her. They were pieces of her dear sister, after all. But now, she suddenly ached for the sight of Zoya's beautiful handwriting, rounded, curvaceous exactly where it should be, the neatly dotted i's and j's and the tiny loops which the y ended in. And for those fine pencil strokes that Zoya made while shading her portraits. Zoya had made sketching look so easy; only when Anya insisted on trying had she realised that it could be an exercise in restraint and judiciousness. "Anni, soft and gentle will get you the best results." Lesson in art, or life? That was how it was always with Zoya. Metaphors, examples, life lesson, all rolled into one.

Anya ran her hands over the diaries. She told herself she would just look at Zoya's neatly spaced-out, well-formed lettering and wouldn't intrude on her sister's thoughts. Hands trembling, she gingerly opened one of the diaries to a random page. It was a sketch. The side profile of a woman with a sombre face and a piercing pensiveness in her eyes. She flipped the pages. More sketches. More women. Some with a scarf around their neck; some in trousers and others with a flowing dupatta. The diary was from when Zoya was in senior school. Whenever anyone would see Zoya's artwork, they would assume that she had inherited her mother's interest in fashion. But now it dawned on Anya that these sketches were Zoya's expression of her sexuality. Her coming out to herself. She tried to imagine how difficult that phase would have been for Zoya. Since Zoya's trip to India—*last* trip to India—Anya had revisited so much of Zoya's life and decisions. Zoya's decision to move out of India was one of these. What everyone had interpreted as ambition was a quest to find a safe space where she could be herself. And it had been the right decision because that was where Zoya had found Laura's love.

Anya reached for another diary. Random jottings, sketching, mundane moments, special celebrations—there was a peek into whatever had touched Zoya when she was writing on these pages.

And then suddenly, the flood of tears came. Anya cried. For Zoya. For Laura. For herself. For her parents. She didn't stop. She cried. For the moments they had memories of. For the moments they would never make memories of again. The tears would stop suddenly. Just when she thought that there were none left, they would come again, as if they had been refilled by the infinite source that her grief was.

She didn't go back to the notebooks. Instead, she opened her email, typed Laura, and began searching. Laura had written to her often, especially in those initial days. The mails were about Zoya (of course!) and would leave Anya angry, distressed, sad—usually all at the same time. She had not read many of them, had deleted some without even opening, or archived others. She hadn't replied to a single one, and the mails had dwindled over time. Anya hadn't been able to understand why Laura had written to her. After all, they hardly knew each other.

As window after window flashed on the screen, Anya began to read the mails without bothering to look at the dates they had been sent on. It didn't matter. Nothing about grieving was linear. What difference could the chronological sequence of emails make to the whirling tornado of emotions that enveloped her whenever she thought about Zoya? From intense anger to the depths of sorrow, from numbness to raging fury, from a wish to dissolve in her own tears to stoically putting on a brave front, Anya always found herself oscillating between extremes. It felt as if she was standing across a huge Ferris wheel, the needle of which would swing between these confusing, conflicting, and intense emotions before settling on the one she least expected. Then just when Anya would make her peace with the feelings and try and get through her day, the needle would swing again, leaving her struggling with her emotions.

It was clear that this was true for Laura also.

'Dear Anni,

I hope you don't mind me calling you that. That's what Zoya always called you, and I can't imagine you with any other name.'

'The memories of our India trip are all I have. It was the happiest time of our life together.'

'How much I miss your Zoydi. You can't imagine how much she meant to me! Or perhaps you are the only one who

can. Because you and me, we were the people she cared for most deeply.'

There it was. The intangible, yet profound link between Anya and Laura—their love for Zoya. And the grief of losing her that had left them forever united. It was a bond forged in love and sealed by grief.

'I will never write again. I will stop teaching my journalism class too. Writing is meaningless without Zoya. Maybe I will switch careers to something which doesn't remind me of the time I spent with Zoya.'

'Anni, I feel so guilty. The vacation to Florida was my idea. If I hadn't insisted on the holiday, Zoya would have been alive today.'

Anya clicked on a couple of more emails.

'Anni, there is a huge hole in my heart, a void that will never fill.'

'Everything feels pointless. Everything is pointless'.

'Anni, I don't want this void to ever be filled. Because it is all that I have left of Zoya.'

'Today, I returned to teach my journalism course. One of my old students just asked me how I was doing? And I felt rage build up in me! What a dumb question! What did she expect me to say? Was I to say, I am fine, which would be the biggest untruth ever? Or did she want me to tell her how I really felt—which is mostly, and at best, a state of mind-numbing sorrow?'

'Why do people who want to console us say dumb things like Zoya is in better place? I am seething with anger.'

'Anni, I have started writing again. For days, I would switch on my computer, open the manuscript, and just look

at the screen, but today, I wrote! I began work on my book again. I think it is what Zoya would have wanted. The book, if I do finish it, will be meaningless without her, but I shall write anyway.'

'It hurts so much to hear the word, India. If this was a physical letter, I won't be able to put the word down on paper. It will forever remind me of Zoya.'

Anya was reading the mails and clicking on more almost maniacally. Windows kept popping up, and her eyes didn't leave the screen for a moment.

'Sometimes, for a few fleeting moments, I feel that my grief and my love for Zoya, are sitting close to each other in my heart. That they are two sides of a coin—one cannot be without the other.'

'Maybe someday I will visit India, or you will visit America. Maybe we will sit and talk about Zoya together. Or maybe we will just burst into tears and not be able to bring Zoya's name to our lips.'

Anya was so intent on her task that she was unaware of the loud piercing guttural sound of despair that was filling the room. Emanating from her own self, it was a lament of loss that she had not allowed herself to express fully until now. But now, there was no stopping. She curled up on the floor and continued to cry.

After a while, she began typing.

'Laura,

Hi

I am working as an emergency physician at a new hospital in Goa. It is a lovely hospital in a beautiful city. And it has a dedicated maternity wing too!

She wrote. And wrote. About the patients she had seen. About Pedro. About her days in the ER. About the Goan bread. She didn't write about loving, losing or missing Zoya. Of coping, hurting or sadness. Because what was felt and understood didn't need to be said. Then, just before ending her mail, she paused.

'I do hope you will continue to write. You are right. That is what Zoydi would have wanted you to do.

Love

Anni'

And then she cried herself to sleep.

Meanwhile, when Anya and Roy had left after the beach barbeque, Neel decided to take a walk. The darkness was illuminated by the moonshine. He walked to the accompaniment of the sounds of the waves crashing at the rocky shores. The trip home had been a time of mixed emotions.

He had not minded his parents' company—he had actually enjoyed it too. He had felt comfortable, understood and accepted for being himself. Most importantly, he had not felt burdened by a need to always receive their approval. But he had stopped short of telling them that he had been selected to the most prestigious Institute for Culinary Sciences in Dehradun. He was aware that this opportunity may not come again. But he was also learning that chasing dreams and making life changing decisions took a lot of courage.

He began walking back to the campus, waving at Grace who was closing Pedro's store on the way.

"Neel, I have shared some changes in the menu with you on email. Do check it when you have the time."

"Hey, let's check it out now."

Just a few minutes later, Neel was completely engrossed in the menu that Nimbus would serve. Sitting on the porch outside the store, reading from his phone under the yellow glow of the lampposts, he was imagining how each dish could be presented. An hour later, he had finished his animated discussion with Grace, when another email dropped. It was Dr Kini, reminding him about the income tax enquiry she was stuck with. Neel groaned. Last week, Dr Kini had requested him to help her with some matters related to her late husband's tax accounts. Of course, as with everything related to accounts, it had been relegated to the back of his mind. He quickly replied apologising for the delay and made his way back to the apartment. Tomorrow was a Sunday and he promised himself to look at the statements that Dr Kini had forwarded him.

28

Cloves and Kokum

The next morning, over the usual breakfast at Bordello's, Neel quickly made notes from Dr Kini's emails. Her late husband's accounts were quite disorganised—something that didn't surprise him. Doctors, he knew, were experts in neglecting both their finances and their health. There were some entries which he would need Dr Kini to clarify before he could prepare the final accounts. He dialled her number.

The phone went unanswered for a while, and he was just about to hang up when he heard Dr Kini's voice at the other end.

"Hello Neel." She sounded tired.

"Dr Kini, I was going over your emails. There are some entries in the statements which I am not clear about. Could I swing by so that you could help me with those?"

Dr Kini's home was tucked away in one of the greenest areas of Goa, and she answered the door almost immediately. She led Neel to the study where the sheer curtains were filtering the sunlight. Her laptop and a sheaf of print outs awaited them on the large mahogany table. Neel's phone call had been a welcome diversion from her thoughts, and she had finally snapped out of the gloominess that she found herself in as Christmas drew nearer.

Neel took in the bare tree in the foyer and the Christmas ornaments on the table beside it—many of them still wrapped in newspaper. He could imagine them being packed lovingly year after year. The tree was quite tall; and there was no way someone as petite as Dr Kini could have placed the shimmery silver star on top. *Must be her husband who had passed away earlier this year*, thought Neel.

Dr Kini returned with a strong, freshly roasted brew and they quickly went over the statements.

When they were done, Neel gently suggested, "Ma'am, if you don't mind, can I help decorate the tree?"

"Oh! I am not sure I would want to do that. I was thinking of giving Christmas celebrations a miss this year."

The tree and the ornaments told Neel a different story.

Malathi looked away. Each ornament brought memories of her late husband, Brigadier Samuel, who had passed away earlier that year. They had always decorated the tree together. He would have been very disheartened to see the tree bare.

"Ma'am, the little child in me loves decorating for festivals." Neel turned on his kiddish charm.

"I would have thought a young man like you would have more interesting things to do. But if it's what you really want, it is fine. You must stay for lunch. Fish curry and rice—simple fare that it is, though.

"That would be great."

Neel carefully unwrapped the ornaments to the accompaniment of the sound of cumin and red chillies crackling in the kitchen and the aroma of spices. Food, even when he wasn't cooking or eating it, was nourishing him.

An hour later, when he finally stretched to put the star on top, Dr Kini was standing behind him. She passed him the string to tie the star in place.

"Thank you, ma'am."

"Thank *you*, Neel."

They moved to the dining area where the large accordion windows flooded the room with sunlight. The fish curry, with its perfect blend of tamarind and coconut, was delectable. The king fish was firm, and there was a deep sweetness that was unusual, but very tasty.

"Cloves, ma'am?"

"Yes, Neel. Many people don't use those, but I like to. I wouldn't have expected you to pick that up."

Neel grinned. "You have used kokum for the sourness, right?"

"Yes, Neel. Tamarind and kokum both can be used. I have used kokum as it is more subtle."

Neel smiled.

"Neel, you seem to have a lot of knowledge and natural flair for food. Do you cook?"

"Yes, ma'am. I enjoy it."

As they ate, Dr Kini shared some of the developments planned for H-of-H in the coming few months.

"The hospital is expanding all verticals. Maybe you could be involved more in the finance section? We could organise a training program for you."

"Err. Actually ma'am, I may not be around next year at H-of-H."

"Don't tell me the competition has poached you?"

"No, ma'am. I might be moving on to something entirely different." Neel replied bashfully. "There is this course that I have been thinking of doing for some time now. Maybe I will finally take the plunge."

"I don't know what it is that you are planning, Neel. But if it makes your eyes sparkle the way they did in our conversation about kokum and cloves, you must do it."

Neel smiled. The delicious curry mixed with rice seemed to have filled more than his stomach and his senses. When he left Dr Kini's home, it was with a feeling of knowing what would satisfy his soul too. The irony that it was accounts and ledgers that had taken him to the place where he finally found the conviction to say yes to himself and overcome his fear was something that his father would point out to him much later.

29

Decisions

The room was tinged with white incandescent light from the projector. Roy looked at Naik's brows knitted in concentration as he spoke.

While the others filed out after the meeting, Naik motioned Roy to stay back.

"So, have you decided anything about my proposal?"

"I am thinking about it," Roy replied.

Vijayant Naik had noted Roy's natural flair for problem solving. That, and his ability to remain composed under pressure, made him an asset in a crisis—and an excellent administrator. He had offered Roy the position of Chief Administrator at H-of-H. But he was also aware of Roy's credentials as a surgeon. This world of files and paperwork was far removed from the excitement of the surgery suite. Even though Roy had never really spoken about the reasons for his joining hospital administration, Naik suspected that the motivation behind this change of streams had its roots in emotional turmoil. To Naik, who had as much experience in understanding people as he did hospitals, it was obvious that there was something that was not quite right with his mentee. The senior doctor was holding space for Roy and simultaneously nudging him towards the next phase of his career, and towards his growth. Whatever course Roy would take—to continue here, or to return to trauma surgery—there was no doubt that a brilliant career awaited him. The only thing missing was a sense of self-assurance.

Vijayant's offer had taken Roy by surprise. Being in the OR, saving lives with his swiftness and precision was what he thrived on. It had been a huge setback when he had begun to doubt his own skill; but he had managed to put that behind him in the last few months. His forays into the OR had increased, and so had his belief in himself. He was working on techniques to conquer the anxiety that he knew would accompany his return to scrubs and scalpels. Compared to that life, the Excel sheets and meetings were humdrum for sure. But then again, he was liking his life here at H-to-H, with Anya and Neel around. After months, he felt a sense of stability inside of him. He felt less of the self-loathing that had become his frequent shadow. That was why he didn't reject Naik's suggestion outright.

It was late evening, but Roy went to this office. He needed to take care of some emails. Once he was done, he began surfing the web to check the status of his applications for fellowship programmes in the US. All the programmes would start in spring of the new year and acceptances were being sent. He hadn't received any. The sudden break in his surgery career was a definite blip on his resume. He wondered what the future would bring.

To distract himself, he began scrolling through their group chat. There were loads of pictures, especially from their beach outings. Most of the pictures had been taken by Neel, and of course, featured clouds. Roy paused at one of the pictures, which was so typical of Neel. The white irregular outlines had been tamed by the pen marker tool, and Neel had given it liquidy blue eyes and a red blobby nose. The cloud now looked like a teddy bear. Anya had loved it. Next was a picture of Anya wearing a large sun hat—bright orange contrasting with the pale pistachio green dress that ended just above her knees. Her sunglasses perched high on the hat, she was walking along the beach, her footsteps on the sand visible behind her. Neel had taken the picture against the mellowness of the setting sun; Roy recalled that evening very well.

They had sat on the beach longer than usual that evening, chatting about their respective college days. Anya had told them how she couldn't bear to think of applying for training abroad again.

"Right now, I can just stay here and look at the ocean forever. I could live in Goa till I am old and grey," she had tried to dismiss the sadness that came with the conversation.

Old, grey and still beautiful, Roy had found himself thinking. Maybe he could also finally put anchor down here; he already had specks of grey anyway. Then he had pushed that thought away.

They had walked along the beach. Then talked and laughed some more. He had wished that life would always be like it was right now. Then he had laughed at himself for having wished for anything. Because his wishes never came true.

Just thinking back to that evening—and many others spent with Anya—made Roy feel warm and fuzzy—and, he realised suddenly, happy. For him, darkness was not just an old friend he bumped into sometimes, but a constant companion. Happiness, on the other hand, was an occasional, fleeting visitor—one that could be so unfamiliar that he failed to recognise it. But, when he was with Anya, he was sure that what he was feeling was happiness. The only problem was that when he felt happy, he also felt like an impostor, as if he didn't deserve the happiness; and that the happiness would be short lived.

He returned to the pictures on his phone.

The last one was of Anya and Roy walking on the beach. Not together. But towards each other. Roy was returning from a walk up to the mountain cliffs. Anya, her earpods in place, had been strolling along the beach. Neel had captured it perfectly—both walking towards each other, the azure of the ocean behind them, and sand glistening in the sun. Roy's eyes and thoughts lingered at the picture.

30

Plans

The trio climbed over the rocks to get to the tiny alcove which had become their favourite spot on the beach.

"I really like the clear water here," Anya said as it washed over her feet.

"Aah yes, one of the many paradoxes of the sea—the clarity despite its layers."

Anya raised her eyebrows on listening to Neel's abstract metaphor.

But before she could say anything, Roy asked. "So, are you all set?"

"For what?"

"Duh, Anya. The New Year's Eve rock concert on Anjuna beach. Have you forgotten we planned that weeks ago?"

"I don't want to go."

Even though she had been in a better head space than earlier about her parents' impending move to Gurgaon, there were times when she could be quite dispirited. The finality of the event was staggering and brought up anguishing memories.

"Anya, this is a signature event. People come from everywhere to Goa just to be a part of this."

Anya didn't reply. "Well, if you don't say yes, I won't let you in on my huge announcement." Neel grinned.

"What announcement?" she asked. Neel sure knew how to pique her curiosity.

"Is this about the secret you have been keeping all these days?" she continued sharply.

Instead of replying, Neel just grinned. Anya was exasperated.

"Tell me, Neel, we have been waiting for so long! What are you up to?"

Anya's impatience made Roy laugh. It was fun watching how Neel had put her in a spot. This was the best way to get her out of the funk she was in, he thought.

And, of course, he was right.

"So, I am blocking the tickets."

But Anya wasn't listening anymore.

"Tell me, Neel, tell me NOW."

They had reached the alcove and Neel had his camera poised at the sky trying to capture the lenticular clouds.

"Don't you think they look like a stack of pancakes?" he turned to Anya.

"I don't care if they look like the entire iHop, Neel. Get on with it, will you?"

"Ok, here goes." Neel knew better than to irk Anya any further.

He took a deep breath and continued. "I have resigned." Anya and Roy looked at Neel's face light up.

"Why?"

"That's big. What's up buddy?"

Anya was already shooting random guesses at him.

"Are you taking a vacation to see the Northern Lights? Have you decided to switch to investment banking?"

Neel was unable to keep his secret from his friends any longer, and he burst out, "I will be joining culinary school at Dehradun. I will be a professional chef. It is something that I have wanted to do for as long as I can remember."

"So that's what you have been hiding all this time! What a big secret! You didn't even tell us that you had applied."

"So happy for you, Neel!"

"There is one more thing...Err...I need to leave in a couple of days."

"Neel, how can this be so sudden?" Anya screamed.

"Anya, I wasn't sure about my decision, so I kept putting off my resignation. But the course begins in a fortnight. Dr Kini put in a word so that I could be relieved immediately."

Once Neel had stopped being indecisive, Dr Kini had insisted he complete the formalities at the earliest. He was grateful to her for having enabled his confidence.

"You really do spring a surprise, Neel." Roy hugged his buddy.

Anya and Roy saw the happiness on Neel's face as they listened to how his visit to Delhi had been a catalyst in this decision and how Dr Kini had gently nudged him towards this step. This was the Neel that he always kept hidden from the world—and from himself.

"That's fantastic!" Anya was thrilled.

"So, we can look forward to your Michelin Star restaurant! Hope you will give a good discount to us."

"I will eat for free." Anya said.

Neel and Roy laughed.

Just like the sunlight from the downing sun glittered on the gently moving waves, Neel's happiness spread to his friends. Anya and Roy chided Neel about his secrecy, congratulated him on his success, and finally hugged and wished him the very best—from their hearts, as only friends can. The reflection of the setting sun in the water below was surrounded by ripples. Like the ripples of joy that was spreading into their hearts. They would ring in the New Year on the beach tomorrow with the rock concert. Then, they would celebrate the New Year with Grace's special dinner menu the day after that.

They walked back with light heartedness and a spring in their step.

Back in his apartment, Roy opened the folder on his computer marked: 'Applications'. Just a day before, he had received a solitary offer confirming his fellowship in surgery. He, who was usually quite sure of himself, was conflicted. With which of the choices was his heart really aligned? Sometimes he longed for the action and pulse of the OR; at other times, he wished life would continue at its steady rhythm here in Goa—where he and Anya were together. The connection he felt with Anya was more than friendship, but he didn't have a name for it. All he knew was that he didn't want it to end. At the same time, how could he throw away a great career opportunity for something that he couldn't even put into words? Whatever his feelings were, he had to be realistic. He was not the sorts who would be lucky in love. He opened the folder and began to type out his acceptance; not allowing himself to get distracted. There were two forms—one for acceptance of the offer, and the other one for selecting the location of the hospital he wanted to train in. He had just completed the first one when he was interrupted by an urgent call from Vijayant—there had been a fire at a hotel some distance away, and the victims were being brought into H-of-H. It was an all-hands-on-deck situation.

As soon as Anya went to her room, she checked the time. It was almost 8 o'clock. In Boston, Laura would be awake.

"Hi Anni, how's everything?"

"Laura, there is something I want to ask you."

"Yes, Anni?"

"Laura, as you know, I didn't send out any applications for the residency programme this year."

"It's ok. Don't stress it. Maybe you weren't ready for it."

This was exactly what Zoya would have said. Zoya and Laura really were soulmates. *Had been* soulmates.

Laura waited. She knew there was something Anya needed help with.

"Laura, you know, the programme that I was applying for before…?"

"Yes, of course Anni, I know about it."

"Well, they are offering places on priority to the applicants who were selected previously but didn't join. I received an email from them a few days back."

Laura was stunned into silence. Zoya had been Anya's guiding light and she would have been so proud to learn of this development.

"Anni, what's bothering you?"

"Laura, I don't know what I want to do."

Anya had wanted this so much at one point of time. But that was another life. This was a great opportunity, one that Zoya had handpicked for her little sister. On the other hand, Anya couldn't find much to complain about her life here at H-of-H either.

Laura understood the conflict without Anya having to spell it out. After all, everything in her own life was touched with Zoya and her memories too. She let Anya sit with her feelings.

But there was something else that Anya hadn't spoken about. At least sometimes, here in Goa, Anya felt calm and happy. And a part of her wished life would always be this way—with Roy around. But that was just wishful thinking. And she, Anya, should know that nothing in life happens the way we expect it to. She didn't know what Roy's plans were. And she wasn't sure if what they shared was friendship or something deeper.

Laura wished she could reach out and hug Anya.

"Anni. What is stopping you from deciding?"

"What do you usually do when you find yourself in conflict?"

"I ask Zoya what to do."

Laura's eyes welled up, but she knew she had to soldier on.

"Well, Anni, Zoya lives on in you. You just have to ask yourself."

Anya steeled herself, and in her head, asked herself what she wanted. What would Zoya have replied if Anya had shared her dilemma with her. But nothing happened. She was suddenly angry. What had she been expecting? Zoya was not here. Not anymore. *And would never be here, either.* Why was she doing this senseless exercise? Then, because she couldn't think of anything else, she repeated the question to herself—this time saying it aloud. And there it was.

"Anni...this is serendipity. It's the same programme that you were applying for. Maybe it's meant to be?"

Anya heard Zoya's voice. Soft and gentle, but unwavering. Anya knew what to do, and she began typing.

She would miss Goa. And Neel. And Roy, of course. She would miss Roy the most. But she couldn't afford to lose out on this opportunity.

She had just pressed send when her phone rang. It was the hospital. Victims from a fire were being brought in.

Neel, too, returned to his room and sat on the couch, thoughts swirling in his head. He was, of course, excited about the future. But there was also a tinge of nervousness. His decision would bring many unknowns, but then even the clouds he loved to watch didn't have a fixed destination. Just as the clouds faced their challenges of uncertain winds and temperature, he too would deal with whatever would come his way. Not following his dream would have brought regret—and that was a heavier burden to carry. In this moment, all he knew was that this was the only choice that seemed to be the right one. And, for the first time in his life, that seemed assurance enough. He was ready for the course, the move to Dehradun, and for being a student again. He would face each challenge when it came, he told himself.

Then his phone rang. "Mass causalities," the voice on the other end said.

31

Firefighting

There was mayhem in the hospital. Bystanders and media were crowding the entrance. The driveway was a picture of chaos with ambulances haphazardly parked and people milling all around. But Roy's discerning eyes noted that the triage teams were already operational. Naik was there too, shooting off instructions. He acknowledged Roy's presence with a terse nod. "Report to Rodrigues in ER. Stat."

Everyone knew it was just the beginning.

In the ER as Roy's eyes searched for Rodrigues, his thoughts raced back to different moments in his career. Despite having worked in the toughest of situations, he felt grossly unprepared for what was unfolding around him.

"Roy, there are three surgical teams. You will lead the one for patients with a combination of burns and trauma."

Roy nodded to Rodrigues. These were the most complicated patients. Across the ER, he saw Anya already there in her scrubs. Their eyes met for a moment before she returned to the patient she was stabilising and he rushed to change into his scrubs. Then, before jumping head first into his onerous task, he repeated the two most important lessons he had learnt in his life to himself. The first was 'Prioritise'. That was how Naik had summarised the entire hospital administration course. And the second one was 'Breathe'. That was what his father had told him whenever he would be having one of his allergy attacks. He hoped he would be able put those two little big words to use when it mattered the most.

For Anya, decision making and caring for multiple patients simultaneously was part of the job. But right now, the ER was akin to a war zone. The burns of her last patient had been more severe than the triage team had recorded, and the patient had decompensated. The lady before that tried to jump off a balcony to save herself from the fire and had compound fractures. Anya had finally managed to get the patient on the orthopaedic surgery list after frantically checking blood availability in the blood bank. A young woman had succumbed to the smoke in her lungs. Anya moved to the next patient—a man in his fifties who was visibly uncomfortable. He had been brought in with asphyxia and burns on his face and had been successfully resuscitated. But, now, his oxygen saturation had suddenly dropped. She quickly turned to Miriam who already had an endotracheal tube ready and took the tube from her and proceeded to intubate the patient. To her dismay, she wasn't able to pass the tube.

"Difficult airway." It was Roy behind her.

It wasn't a question. It was a statement—difficult airway was a technical term in medicine.

She nodded. "There doesn't seem to be airway injury."

"Oedema?" A laryngoscopy would have helped, but there was no time for one, Roy mused.

"When did the fire breakout?" Anya replied with a question of her own.

"Around 8 last night."

Roy looked at his watch and immediately understood what Anya meant. It was almost 4 am. Then, he examined the patient's burns more closely. They were extending to the neck.

The burns were superficial but the dead tissue was pressing the neck from outside. Any intervention that Anya tried inside the airway would fail.

"Drapes," he called.

Once the area was sterile, he quickly infiltrated local anaesthetic.

"Are you doing an escharotomy?"

"Yes."

Anya didn't ask him if he had ever done one before. He had, but just once, and that been on the leg. Yet, he knew that he didn't have a choice if he wanted to give the patient a chance.

In one defining stroke of his scalpel, Roy proceeded to remove the tissue that had begun to stiffen. He needed to be very careful to avoid the jugular and carotids. He hoped he was doing the right thing the right way. And just a few moments later, he saw his incision immediately bulge open—a sign of success.

Anya relaxed as the oxygen saturation began to stabilise. Despite the situation they were working in, both managed a small smile. A win was a win. They needed to acknowledge it, even savour it to give themselves the strength to trudge along.

"Want to take a coffee break?"

Anya looked doubtful.

"I think we need it, Anya." Roy continued.

They had been on their feet for more than eight hours.

"Miriam. We are stepping out for a moment."

They headed to the coffee machine.

They sat on the couch and looked outside from the windows. The chaos outside had settled down, but the situation inside the hospital would take a while. Anya's long sips of coffee gave her strength to take small bites of the sandwich. Roy avoided the food—he was hungry, but he couldn't risk falling ill. He rested his head on Anya's shoulder and shut his eyes for a few moments.

Within 10 minutes they were back in the ER.

A few of Anya's patients had been shifted into the ICU and she went there to take rounds. Roy was paged to the OR for what he knew would be a long session.

It was almost 24 hours now since Anya and Roy had rushed to the hospital. No new patients were being brought in and a sense of exhaustion was replacing the urgency that they had felt all around them.

The doctors, nurses and paramedics had worked without being aware of how much time had passed. They ate when they could, stole a nap when they were too fired to function anymore, and sneaked out for coffee or a nibble in between rounds.

Exhausted and having done what they could, Anya and Roy left for their apartments. Meanwhile, outside, the sun was setting not just on the day, but on an entire year. Everyone would be preparing for an evening of merriment.

32

Sharing News

After returning to their apartments, Roy fought the fatigue long enough to check the internet for press coverage of the fire incident, but finally succumbed to sleep. Anya was too tired to even walk to her bed and had slept off on the couch.

Dawn, and a new year crept up on them, but they slept on, oblivious.

The night of the fire, Neel had helped the triage teams in the reception bay and had returned home earlier.

Neel knew his friends would be exhausted, so he was putting together cheese boards for them. He neatly arranged the cheese and olives, and then seasoned the roasted chickpeas. He added sourdough to Anya's and bananas to Roy's platter. Not wanting to wake them up, he texted them and left the cling film-wrapped platters outside their doors.

Anya woke up around 2 pm and savoured the platter before showering.

"The platter is awesome, Neel."

Roy, meanwhile, slept in till 4 pm.

"Thanks Neel. I was starving."

"Catch up at the beach in the evening, before going to Nimbus for dinner?" Neel texted back.

Grace had been preparing for weeks for the New Year special. Tired as they were, they knew they couldn't disappoint her.

"Let's meet at our spot." Anya typed back quickly.

"Yeah! We didn't even get around to celebrating your news that day!"

Roy was glad that his usually ambivalent friend had finally decided to follow his dream. And what better way to celebrate than at Grace's new restaurant?

He parked his bike at the end of the small road, and began walking to the beach, thinking of the many times he had come here with Anya—mostly riding pillion because Anya always preferred to be on the driver's seat. It was something that he didn't mind; he liked the feeling of closeness that it brought. Just like the many walks they took on the beach, sometimes holding hands. He had got Anya to try jogging on the beach, something that wasn't easy to get the hang of. But she had caught on quickly and could even outrun him. How quickly they had become friends, despite their initial frosty interaction on his first day at the hospital, he thought and smiled.

Those conversations they had had into the night when she was in Delhi were the longest he had ever had with anyone. He would have left Goa by now if it hadn't been for their walks on the beach to look forward to after those boring administrative meetings. For so long, he had stopped himself from thinking about their kiss the other night, but now suddenly, all the feelings that it had stirred up were resurfacing. In the hospital yesterday, they had worked in complete harmony, exchanging glances across the crowded ER, their eyes meeting in unsaid understanding. In addition to the chemistry that he tried to sweep under the carpet of his reclusiveness, there was a kinship and understanding that he had never experienced with anyone else. He was finally sure that he was ready to take their relationship beyond the 'friends' space it had occupied till now. He had resisted the thoughts for so long because of the baggage he carried from his relationship with Denise, but he finally felt ready to put those ghosts to rest. He stopped at the first shack on the beach and picked up Anya's favourite beer before walking on to their regular spot.

Even though Anya had showered and washed her hair, the feeling of soot seemed to cling to her body. No matter how much experience she, or any other doctor had, they could never be desensitised from tragedies. But she also knew that dwelling on it was not going to help. She stood in front of her wardrobe and looked for something that would make her feel fresh.

She decided on a crop top and shorts. Hoping to leave the gruelling sights and smells of the horrific tragedy behind her, she splashed some perfume with a strong floral note (Zoya's favourite brand) on her pulse points.

She walked to the beach, thinking about Neel's decision. Though she was still mad at him for keeping it a secret for so long, she was also thrilled for him. She was sure he would become a famous chef.

Of course, she would miss him. It had been a quick and effortless friendship, one that was rare in adulthood. Later, despite her initial misimpressions, Roy had become a friend too. There had always been a sense of reserve around him, and she had got to know him gradually. Then, when she had visited his home in Delhi, she had understood him better. She couldn't deny the attraction that she had felt for him on at least a few occasions. In the many hours they had spent with each other on the beach and in the hospital, she had felt a connection. The one time that they had kissed had been surreal. Did this feeling not transcend the boundary between friendship and love?

Dusk had begun to fall. The sky was a multitude of colours, the reflection of which shone in the waves below. Silhouettes of the paragliders against the setting sun could be seen.

By the time Anya reached the beach, Neel and Roy had set up the bluetooth speaker.

"Hi Anya, we just got here."

"My playlist?"

Neel laughed. She wouldn't let it be any other way. "Of course."

Roy couldn't take his eyes off Anya. Her curly hair was falling on her face. She looked beautiful in the yellow crop top and denim shorts.

"Beer?"

She nodded and he took out a can from his duffel bag, his hand brushing against hers. In that moment, Roy wished he could always be here on the beach with her. He then shook his head with exasperation. The little boy in him needed to be content with collecting seashells instead of entertaining such frivolous thoughts.

Anya sat down on the sand near the shore. She ran her fingers in the sand, letting some of the grainy particles stick to her fingers while the rest was washed away. In that moment, she felt the fragile calmness that she had begun to experience only in the last few months in Goa. *If only this moment could last forever,* she thought to herself. But she knew better than her anyone how fleeting the tranquil moments of life could be.

Neel and Roy joined her on the sand. The friends listened to the silence and took in the view. They were all thinking back to the last time they had sat here—just two days ago, when Neel had shared his news about culinary school. It was hard to believe that 48 hours ago, they had been making plans to attend a music concert. All of that had been eclipsed by the tragedy that unfolded at a resort where tourists had been booked in for the New Year revelry. How things could change in a moment.

In those hours at the hospital, this beach had seemed a lifetime away. Now, that seemed to be eons ago. Existing in parallel, both were real and true.

Amid this shared silence and similar reflections, Anya and Roy finally found the headspace to grasp what they had been doing just before the calls about the fire accident had come in. The emails that they had been reading and had replied to came to mind. They looked at each other and held the other's gaze. The decisions they had made flashed through their minds; their meanings and implications now becoming clear. It wasn't just Neel whose life had seen major developments that evening. Both of them had taken huge leaps forward in their career just before those calls.

Roy cleared his throat.

"Actually, I have something to share too."

Neel looked surprised.

"I always pretended that I was doing hospital management for a change. But the truth is that I was worried that I didn't have it in me to be a surgeon anymore. That I couldn't make the cut—both literally and figuratively."

Anya was stunned. How could Roy not be a surgeon?

"A breakup with my girlfriend Denise affected me so much that I made a huge mistake in the OR, risking my patient's life. I lost confidence in my capability. But now, I am finally putting that behind me. but I finally overcame my fears to apply for training programmes in America. I have been accepted for the programme."

"That is super, Roy." Neel slapped him on the back.

Anya was still taking it all in. She had wondered about the reason behind his self-imposed hiatus from the OR, but she had never imagined that his fears ran so deep.

"Congratulations!"

"Thanks. This is a very coveted programme, and I am lucky to have made it."

"No Roy, you deserve this." Anya assured him.

"I also have something to tell you." Anya continued.

"So, before Zoya's death…" Anya's voice faltered a bit when she took her sister's name. "I had been planning to train in critical care medicine. Zoya had been helping me with my applications. But after…everything that happened, I never got around to joining even though I had been selected for a prestigious programme in Philadelphia. This year, I thought of applying again, but…didn't. I just couldn't…"

Neel put his arm around her shoulder.

"But, based on my previous application, the programme has offered me a place."

Roy and Neel waited. Both knew that this must have opened a Pandora's Box of emotions. Roy slipped his hand in hers.

"I accepted," she said, softly.

Roy squeezed her hand. Neel hugged her and pulled Roy into the huddle too.

"This calls for champagne! I wish we had brought some." Neel exclaimed.

"Isn't it a great coincidence that all of us are starting afresh at the same time?" Roy asked.

Anya spoke before Neel could reply. "It is more than just happenchance. I think it's meant to be. Maybe coming to Goa when we did and becoming friends, was what we were meant to do. Maybe it is serendipity at work? The universe doing what we trusted it to?" Anya surprised herself with her own words. This was what Zoya would have said.

Once again, Anya and Roy's eyes locked. Both felt that chemistry. They couldn't deny it had existed—that it still did. And that they liked it and wanted to feel again. But they had both taken decisions that would take them away from each other.

Their hearts had filled with joy just a moment ago, but now it was the turn of their eyes to turn moist. They looked away from each other, grappling with the paradox of this emotional roller coaster.

So many developments, so many changes and myriad feelings—it was a whirlwind.

Must serendipity also come with this sense of loss? Would the universe always cheat them of a little something even when it pretended to bestow upon them its blessings? Was this how their trust in the universe would be rewarded? Must they always find a flawed and blemished happiness?

Their eyes met again. As their gaze locked, they felt a wordless pact forming between them. Both were no strangers to heartache, and they would confront their pain later. They would not allow unhappiness to intrude on this beautiful evening. In this moment they would hold on to the beauty they saw and the beatitude they felt. They waited for the sun to go down.

A while later, Neel who had been exploring new angles for his photographs reminded them. "Let's get going for dinner."

"Yes, let's go. I will come back later to pick up my bike."

33

Moonshine

The ambience of the restaurant was enchanting. A large alfresco seating area complemented the indoor area which had a slated bamboo ceiling. Greens peppered both areas. The restaurant had a soothing vibe. The flames of the candles on the tables flickered. Grace welcomed them with hugs, and led them to the terrace, where the inviting cabanas were lit up with soft yellow lights. She was in her element as she personally selected the menu for her friends, being extra careful about Roy's preferences.

Once they were done with starters, Neel quickly made excuses to check out the kitchen, much to his friends' amusement.

Anya and Roy, who had both struggled with conflicting emotions just a little while ago, surrendered to the foot-tapping music that streamed from the speakers. The lights on the potted plants gave it a magical feeling—as if fairy dust had been sprinkled around them. In those moments, the past seemed to be at a remote distance. And the future was too far ahead for them to dwell upon. It was just them, and their now. They relaxed and enjoyed the food, the weather and the view.

It was when they were having dinner that Roy's phone buzzed. Expecting it to be a message from Naik about the hospital, he reached for his phone. It was an email, from the Williamson General Hospital. He had missed submitting his city option in his last mail. There were five cities which he could choose from—Boston, New York, Seattle, Virginia, and Philadelphia. Roy was bewildered, but only for a moment. Then a feeling of tranquillity washed over him, an inner calmness that matched the serenity of his surroundings. He savoured the feeling as much as the food.

It was when Anya was digging into a sizzling brownie that he finally spoke, "Philadelphia, right?"

"Huh?"

"Anya, you said you are going to Philadelphia, right?"

"Yes, Roy, I am. Oh! I never got around to asking you where you have signed up for your training."

Roy silently studied his ice cream.

"Roy, what is your problem? First Neel and now you—why is everyone keeping secrets?" Anya was getting irritated, but Roy didn't try to calm her down. Instead, he walked to the edge of the terrace and looked out into the distance. Anya quickly finished her brownie and joined him. He took out his phone.

"Roy, I asked you a simple question, but, as usual you are busy with your phone."

Ignoring Anya's impending flare-up, Roy opened his inbox. Then, he quickly sent the shortest—and most pivotal—email of his life before holding his phone out for Anya to read.

"Philadelphia," he said, almost inaudibly.

Anya looked at Roy, unsure of what to make of this.

"You asked where I would be relocating to. It's Philadelphia."

Anya understood.

"It really is serendipity, isn't it?" Anya replied softly and put her hand in his. Roy didn't bother replying.

They came closer and their lips found each other. They kissed—a deep long kiss of longing, belonging and of dreams they could finally dare to see.

It was with much reluctance that they stopped a few moments later when Neel called out to them.

"Hey guys! Have you seen the clear sky? Is that a constellation there?"

The word constellation had Anya's attention, and she looked at the sky.

It was Orion, Zoya's favourite constellation that Neel was pointing towards. She felt as if her sister was watching over her.

"Neel, take a picture of us," Roy said.

The picture, like the moment, was perfect. Anya and Roy looked straight ahead, not just at the camera but also towards a new year and a new life. It would become a testimony to the fact that life, despite its brokenness and imperfection, also contained hope and possibility.

As one phase of their life came to a close, a new one was beginning. Because endings are not always final.

Acknowledgements

I would not have had the courage to send another book out into the world if it wasn't for the many people who showered their love on my debut book *Stars from the Borderless Sea*. My heartfelt gratitude for giving me your time and putting your faith in my words.

My family—a comforting constant in the chaos of life—especially my parents and my children. It is their love that always anchors me steadfastly and their perennial encouragement that fuels me when I am running on empty.

My corner which is full of big-hearted people; friends who have celebrated my highs and stood by me in my lows. Thank you Ramanjaneya, Arva, Natasha and Salini for beta reading, reviewing and giving insightful comments which added immense value to this manuscript. And for the single line texts and the long chats, the laughter and the memes, the pep talks and the permissions to slacken. For being exactly what I needed at a particular point in time.

Dipankar, for his belief in my work, his consistent encouragement and pragmatic advice.

Indrani, for her patience, meticulous attention to detail and her enriching inputs.

Lee, for his help with the blurb.

The community that I found through my writing—people who have cheered me from the sidelines, connections that I forged, and precious souls whose values resonate with mine. I cannot list all of you here, but your support truly means a lot to me.

Lastly, you, the reader—for having picked up this book. I hope the words and emotions in these pages touch you.

Shalini Mullick
Gurugram, 2024

About the Author

Shalini is the author of *Stars from the Borderless Sea,* which was longlisted for the AutHer Awards 2023 (Best Debut). The book has also been featured on many websites and platforms like Kitaab.org and Women's Web.

Shalini was awarded a Jury Appreciation Citation at the 12th UNFPA Laadli Media & Advertising Awards for Gender Sensitivity (2022). Her stories on women's identity have won many short story contests and two Orange Flower Awards (Fiction, 2022 and LGBTQ issues, 2021). Five of her short stories have found home in three anthologies. A humorous short story was selected for the Juggernaut Selects program (2020). Her poetry has been published in reputed Medical Humanities journals.

Shalini is known for her insightful, thought provoking and engaging content.

She has been an invited speaker at literary events like the Delhi Literature Festival, Women in Literature Festival, Midnight at Book Store, House of Harmony Spring Festival, Ghaziabad Literature Festival and the Golden Door Dialogues. She is a columnist and panellist for platforms like eShe, Ananke, Beyond the Box, Women's Web and Incredible Women of India. She is regularly invited to prestigious schools and educational institutes for literary and career counselling events. She has also been an invited guest on audio and video podcasts.

Shalini is also a practicing doctor. She is the Head, Department of Pathology, at the National Institute of

Tuberculosis and Respiratory Diseases, Delhi. She has trained and worked at premier institutes and organisations and authored and reviewed many scientific papers and textbook chapters.

Shalini is happiest in the company of books, chocolate and old Hindi movie songs. She loses herself in the melody of ghazals and finds herself in their lyrics. Poetry touches her soul, and she believes there is a perfect Rumi quote for every situation in life.

Though she has beautiful memories of her years in Bangalore and has now put down roots in Gurgaon, Shalini remains a Dilliwali at heart.

You can discover more about her on:
www.shalinimullick.com
Facebook: https://www.facebook.com/shalini.mullick
Instagram: @shalinimullick
X/Twiter: @MullickShalini

Also by Shalini Mullick

Stars from the Borderless Sea

What is true love? Who are soulmates? Can love be defined by the constructs of society and convention? Can an affair rescue a marriage? Can true love ever tear people apart?

Two college mates fall in love, only to be separated-their love stays steady, though they meet just twice in forty years.

A close-knit family, shadows from the past, a lingering suspicion, and a relationship put to the test.

An emotionally unavailable husband, a hurt wife; and an affair that redeems and transforms.

Three strong women, and their journeys. And love, as mature and strong as them. In these times of speed dating, hook-ups and break-ups, Stars from the Borderless Sky, a collection of three riveting stories, takes an unconventional, honest, empathetic look at that most universal of human emotions—love.

Readomania

Readomania exists to nurture, curate, and bring to you content you love. We are a publishing house that takes pride in encouraging talent, new or old, and provide a wonderful platform for awesome stories.

We make this possible in multiple ways.

The first as an independent publishing house. Readomania boasts of multiple imprints across various categories—fiction, nonfiction, children, to name a few. An eclectic mix of content for its readers, when you read a Readomania title, you enter a world that's yours, supported by unique and quality narratives.

The second, as an online publishing platform for writers—a place to share stories, poems, opinions, travelogues, a way to explore your creative talent. Available as premium, as well as free-to-read content across multiple genres, the reader is spoilt for choice.

Join us in this journey, as we explore, develop, and present stories to our readers and audiences. Welcome to the world of Readomania, get ready to craft stories that enrich lives.

You can visit us at: www.readomania.com